MURDER OVER DORVAL

Murder Over Dorval

David Montrose

A RICOCHET BOOK

Véhicule Press

Published with the generous assistance of the Canada
Council for the Arts, the Canada Book Fund of the
Department of Canadian Heritage, and the Société de
développement des entreprises culturelles du Québec
(SODEC).

Adaptation of original cover: J.W. Stewart
Consulting editor: Brian Busby
Special assistance: Claire Grandy
Typeset in Minion by Simon Garamond
Printed by Marquis Printing Inc.

LIBRARY AND ARCHIVES CANADA CATALOGUING
IN PUBLICATION

Montrose, David, 1920-1968
Murder over Dorval / David Montrose.

(Ricochet books ; 2)
Originally publ.: Toronto : Collins, c1952.
ISBN 978-1-55065-291-8

I. Title. II. Series: Ricochet books 2.

PS8526.O593M87 2010   C813'.54   C2010-905337-0

Published by Véhicule Press, Montréal, Québec, Canada
www.vehiculepress.com

Distribution in Canada by LitDistCo
www.litdistco.ca

Distributed in the U.S. by Independent Publishers Group
www.ipgbook.com

Printed in Canada on recycled paper

Publisher's Note (2010)

Murder Over Dorval, published in 1952, has been long out of print. This is the second book in the Véhicule Press Ricochet series. Typos that appeared in the original book have been corrected; the sexist and racist attitudes of the period remain.

Foreword to the 2010 Edition

THE BOOK YOU ARE about to read – or may have already read, saving this Foreword until last – is a prime example of the hardboiled pulp-noir detective fiction of the 1930s, 40s and 50s. The style was popularized by the likes of Americans James M. Cain, Dashiell Hammett, Raymond Chandler, and Mickey Spillane, and carried on in a wide variety of styles by many writers since. But while you have probably heard of Cain, and the others, even if you haven't read any of their books, it's unlikely that you've ever heard of David Montrose, the pen name adopted by Canadian Charles Ross Graham in the early nineteen fifties. Well, neither had I – nor very many others – until very recently.

There's good reason for that. Montrose wrote only four books, all long out of print: *The Crime on Cote des Neiges* (1951), *Murder Over Dorval* (1952), and *The Body on Mount Royal* (1953), featuring Montreal private eye Russell Teed, and *Gambling with Fire* (1969) also set in Montreal, but featuring displaced Austrian aristocrat Franz Loebek. Born in 1920 in New Brunswick, little is known of Montrose's life, and he died in 1968, probably in Toronto, shortly before *Gambling with Fire* was released. He has since faded into almost complete obscurity.

Which is too bad.

It's fair to say that just about everything I learned about writing mysteries came from reading mysteries. My list of favourite authors, living and dead, is long, from Hammett and Chandler through Ross MacDonald and John D. MacDonald to James Lee Burke, Peter Robinson,

Gail Bowen, to name just a very few. And I am constantly adding new writers to the list.

Now I've added David Montrose.

It seems a pretty safe bet that Charles Ross Graham read Raymond Chandler, and perhaps even consciously tried to emulate him. He's no mere epigone, though. Montrose's Russell Teed is more than just a pale imitation of Philip Marlowe. Sure, he's hardboiled, hard-drinking and frequently hard done by, but he is as unique a character as Spillane's Mike Hammer, Ross MacDonald's Lew Archer or John D. MacDonald's Travis McGee.

While Montrose's detective Russell Teed shares much in common with the classic hard-boiled private investigator – a glib, cynical, heavy-drinking loner between 35 and 45, frequently a war veteran and so familiar, sometimes even comfortable, with violence and death – Teed differs from his more famous contemporary counterparts in a couple of important regards. And not simply because he's Canadian and a Montrealer.

Teed isn't quite as cool and tough as Philip Marlowe, nor as philosophical, although he is as prone to a degree of introspection. And he's nowhere near as self-righteous or as brutally violent and misogynistic as Mike Hammer. In fact, while he's capable of employing violence to achieve a resolution to his case, he seems slightly ill at ease about it. He's a talker, not a fighter, but he takes his share of beatings and bullets and comes back for more.

Unlike many other hardboiled types, Teed isn't a product of the mean streets. He grew up in affluent and very English Westmount, although "below The Boulevard." He attended good schools and is comfortable around money, although he is equally comfortable around street-savvy lowlifes. A former newspaperman and corporate wage-slave, Teed used his business experience to set himself up as a financially successful "investigative consultant," specializing in corporate malfeasance. He doesn't often carry a gun, lives in a nice apartment, which he decorated himself, and drives a Riley two-seater roadster. He even cooks, when he has time.

Reading Montrose's novels – as with Hammett's, Chandler's and Spillane's – is like climbing aboard a time machine and being transported to a very different time and place. In Montrose's case, the place is mid-twentieth century Montreal. Russell Teed's Montreal bears little resemblance to the dull, politically correct city of the post-Drapeau, post-Quiet Revolution era. Many of the English street names of the 50s are now gone. With one or two exceptions, the bars and restaurants Teed visits are fictional, but they were based on what is now a long-gone reality.

The oddest thing, though, to anyone familiar with twenty-first century Montreal, is the almost complete absence of French. There isn't a single French character in *Murder Over Dorval*. There was only one French character in *The Crime on Cote des Neiges*, the tough, competent Dt. Sgt. Raoul Framboise, who's been replaced by the tough, competent Inspector John Dorset of the RCMP.

You also have to read Montrose's books – as you also have to read Hammett's, Chandler's and Spillane's – with your internal censors turned off. While Teed isn't openly racist or sexist, he is a product of the times, and his language, although mild, reflects it. Despite the almost laughable dialect and the fact that they are bad guys, the black characters in *Murder Over Dorval* are portrayed with a degree of respect, as is Dt. Sgt. Framboise in *The Crime on Cote des Neiges*. Although Véhicule Press has included a disclaimer warning readers that the racist and sexist attitudes were not edited, it really isn't necessary. Still, the book must be read in the context of the time it was written.

Montrose was a good writer, certainly as good as Chandler or Spillane, and he knew how to craft a story and populate it with interesting characters, although he would have benefited from better editing than he received from his pulp publishers. I believe that if he'd continued writing, he'd have continued to develop and polish his style, possibly becoming as well known as his American contemporaries.

Roger Waters, a founding member of Pink Floyd, once said in an interview that while he wasn't a big fan of the Beatles, if it hadn't been for the Beatles, Pink Floyd wouldn't be playing the music it played. If it weren't for writers like James M. Cain, Dashiell Hammett, Raymond Chandler, and Mickey Spillane, I likely wouldn't be writing the kind of books I write.

Now David Montrose has a place on my bookshelves beside them.

Michael Blair
Montreal, Quebec
September 2010

[Michael Blair's most recent book is *Depth of Field: A Granville Island Mystery*.]

Scene One

GRAND CENTRAL STATION is a great seashore. The tide comes in between eight and nine in the morning, and goes out between five and six in the afternoon, and nothing withstands it. The tide is human, and it flows in from New Jersey and everywhere else commuters commute from, and it inundates Manhattan. It enters office buildings, and if it is male it puts the incoming mail neatly in a pile before it, whereas if it is female it pulls a handle and brings a typewriter into the ready position. Then it flows down elevator shafts for coffee. It comes back and either flips the mail casually into the Out basket or dusts the typewriter, and goes for lunch.

The New York afternoon is usually too hot to permit much effort. The tide (male) contemplates the cute blonde in the opposite skyscraper and wishes New York streets were narrower, or (female) discusses why Mr. Pocahackus, the office bachelor, is so shy. It flows discreetly away for a Coca-Cola. It comes back and either tidies up the desk or pushes the typewriter away. It has then done A Good Day's Work and accumulates in flood-tide proportions in Grand Central Station, whence it ebbs away to New Jersey and wherever else commuters commute to.

This is civilization. Progress. Efficiency. Dynamic twentieth-century living. This is the pattern that has made the wealthiest and tallest city in the world into the richest and highest city in the world, with buildings that intrude on altitudes where an angel riding a small cloud would be dizzy.

It was a fine pattern, if you liked it. If you fitted in. But try to buck the current and all you got were buffets. I was in no condition to be buffeted.

I had been drinking in Montreal before I got foolish. After I got foolish I caught the overnight to New York. I woke up at four a.m. thinking I was going to be sick in my roomette. It was one of the most horrible thoughts I've ever had, but finally I went back to sleep. I woke in Grand Central. I fought my way past the Pullman porter, walked down a dank underground passage about two storeys below Fifth Avenue, up a long ramp, and into the tide. And all because of a girl who claimed to be a redhead.

The tide swept past me in waves, and the grey matter in my head rolled about in waves. There was a small booth ahead that looked like a coffee stand. I concentrated on being washed that way by the tide. After I'd ducked my head through about five breakers, I made it. A cup of black coffee came to me. It had been made by American angels in Heaven.

It was ten years since I'd last been in New York. I was surprised how much I'd changed in that time. I don't think New York had. Ten years back, there were tides. But I was on furlough from training camp, just before I went to Europe, and I enjoyed swimming in rough water then.

Ten years is a long time. It saw me through the war, settled back in Montreal as an investigator, sober, sensible, and not given to impulse. Not given to impulse, except when taken at a disadvantage with my head in a noggin of ale.

That was the way the redhead had found me. She had rung my phone. After this, if I must drink alone, I must get too drunk to answer telephones.

I had another cup of coffee.

The tide ebbed momentarily. I picked up my Gladstone and tottered lopsidedly across that great windswept plain which is the concourse of Grand Central Station. Straight ahead of me all the way across was a great jovial joker in an illuminated, animated sign, monotonously raising a foaming stein of beer to his lips and dropping it again. When I got close enough for him to see me I gagged at him.

After many more nights and days of safari I reached my goal. I ran out of water on the way and my horse got so lame I had to shoot him, but there it was. A big sign with two beautiful words –'Commodore' and 'Bar'. I went in. I put down the Gladstone and got my shoulder back into its socket without an anesthetic. They still had the same morning bartender. I couldn't remember whether his name was Jack or Bill; that's what ten years does. But he was the same one. He was small and scrawny, with a narrow quizzical face and the same kind, understanding look a Newfoundland dog gets in his eyes just before he licks your cheek.

"Good morning, Sir," he said.

"You once gave me some very good advice," I told him. "You told me whiskey sours were the only thing fit to drink at this time of day."

"I'm afraid I don't remember."

"No matter. It was a long time ago. Besides, I never take good advice. I want a beer and a redhead. Make the beer Black Horse, very cold, and make the redhead young, with curves."

He brought a Black Horse pint. I got it away from him and poured it myself, very carefully, tilting the glass so there would be no head. He said, "The redhead should be here any minute."

"How is she?"

"What are you expecting?"

"I'll take what comes. How did you know I was expecting?"

"A lady came to the bar a few minutes ago, just before I unlocked the doors. She was a redhead."

"Good," I said. I sipped. The Black Horse was very cold. "Good," I said again, meaning the beer this time. "Describe."

"A good deal smarter than what you usually see around here at this time of the morning. Maybe she comes from Canada too?"

"All right, be smart," I said. "You pegged me for a Montrealer because I poured my beer properly."

He shook his head smugly. "A lot of New York people have picked up that trick." He pointed to my cigarette pack, lying on the bar. State Express. To make it a plastic pipe cinch, the match folder on top of the cigarettes was advertising the Trafalgar Hotel – Montreal's Better Bar.

I shook my head sadly. "And I'm supposed to be the detective of the pair," I told him.

"Bartenders are better detectives than detectives. They get to know human nature."

"No!" I said, "I hadn't heard."

"When the redhead comes in, she'll order a glass of milk," he told me soberly.

"She'll order a whiskey sour."

He shook his head. "I've seen her."

"If she orders milk, you get paid for a whiskey sour. If she drinks, I get a beer on you."

We shook on it. Then he had to work to get his hand loose, because the redhead was there beside us and I forgot him. I forgot feeling mewly in my roomette. I forgot the Grand Central tide. I was glad I'd come. If she'd sent me a picture, I would have come to Minsk to see her.

She had said on the phone that I would know her because she had red hair. She was right. I would have gone straight to her through a whole chorus line of standard redheads, because they would seem faded to dull brown or spoiled blonde beside her. Her hair was long and rich and thick and red as a sunset before a storm, red as the facets of a ruby, red as fresh arterial blood.

She set off the hair with a big, halo-like white hat that framed her face and broadened it. It was an unconventionally beautiful face — long, with wide eyes, a grand straight sweep of nose, smooth flat cheek planes with the color of her creamy skin shading delicately across them, a mouth not too wide with lips not too full, yet decidedly not thin.

She wore a plain, exquisitely-cut dress of very dark, live green. It was of some loosely-woven material, crisp-looking and yet with a sheer drape that faithfully modeled the curves of her lissome body. She was a slim, lithe woman with hips only a little wider than her shoulders. She looked as though she could move at any required rate of speed under the worst conditions of temperature and humidity, without overheating. Her breasts were small for the current fashion, but she had resisted the Hollywood pressure to pad and primp them. They were not the Venus de Milo appendages to a matchstick body that girls buy today in every store. They were breasts slim as her body was slim, high and beautifully shaped and excitingly pointed.

The bartender said, "Yes, Miss?"

She smiled at him. She had bands on her teeth.

You meet all types. The redhead was no little girl — I'd say she was on the interesting side of twenty-five. But she had bands on her teeth, like Susie Smith in the fifth grade at Roslyn School. The teeth must have been going through the straightening process for years — they were nice, straight white teeth. But you could hardly see them for the bands.

She wasn't self-conscious about them. She saw me stare. She went right on smiling. "Milk, please, if you serve it," she told the bartender.

So I was a failure. I didn't know human nature. More than that, I was a foolish failure. I had been plucked from a satisfactory Montreal life, dropped in the middle of milling Manhattan mobs, and I didn't know human nature from a hole in the basement floor. I didn't know milk from whiskey. So how could I help this troubled wench? And if I couldn't help her, I shouldn't have come.

Maybe I didn't know milk from whiskey, but I knew a good morning drink. I told the bartender, "Put me on the milk list too. And spill about three ounces of Teacher's Highland Cream in the bottom of the glass."

So long as I was a foolish failure, I would see to it I was a drunk foolish failure.

Troubled wench? The redhead had sounded troubled over the telephone. She'd sounded desperate. Now she looked about as desperate as a kitten lying asleep by the fireplace.

"Thank you for coming," she said. Her voice was high and sweet, not shrill. I'll bet she sang a true soprano. Her bands flashed gleaming silver at me. She was smiling.

I said sourly, "You seem very calm this morning. Are you sure you wanted me? What did I come for?"

"This," she said. She opened her white handbag and groped. She began laying money on the bar in front of me. The bills made a crisp, neat, sweet little pile; ten one-hundred dollar bills, U.S. currency.

If you want to rouse a Canadian's cupidity, show him United States hundred dollar bills. There's something about them. They're not any better than Canadian hundred dollar bills; they're just a little scarcer, a little more esoteric. I loved them.

I let my fingertips caress the bills. They felt cool and smooth and substantial. "I see," I said. "Well, it was almost worth the trip, to see these. And touch them. Too bad it's not my kind of job."

"You haven't heard about it yet."

"I don't have to. My work doesn't pay this kind of money. People get the wrong idea about me, because I have a private investigator's license. But I operate within the law, not outside it. I don't work on evidence for divorce suits. And I don't care who you want killed, I won't kill him for you. Not for ten times that much. Probably not for twenty times."

"I was told your fees were high. That's why I came prepared. I can afford not to quibble."

"But I can't afford to be bribed. Sure, my fees are high. I do nice, respectable jobs for big corporations, mostly. I find out how the Secretary-Treasurer managed to buy a house and two Cadillacs without dipping into his salary or shooting himself after the annual audit. I enquire into expense accounts that show business trips to England when they really mean passage for two to Bermuda. And I do a lot of less exciting things like fingering industrial spies and tracing missing accountants. Businessmen in Montreal consider me an expert, a consultant, and consulting fees come high. When I finish a job I submit a neat little bill and I get a neat little cheque. But nobody ever comes in, plunks a grand in front of me, and asks me to commit something for them."

She colored. Color was attractive to her cream complexion. "I don't want you to commit anything," she protested.

"Then stop throwing all those beautiful marbles around, because you clearly don't know the value of money. Put it away." I shoved it at her. It burnt my fingers where they touched it.

She put the money back in her purse, slowly, reluctantly.

Her face was longer than a rainy weekend in the

country. "You won't take the job," she said. Flatly, not as a question. She was easy to discourage.

"I don't like the sound of it. But," I said cheerfully, "tell me. Maybe I have the wrong impression." Maybe that would brighten her up. I wanted her to smile again. I wanted to see those bands. I'd never known a grown woman with bands on her teeth, and they began to intrigue me. Thinking it over and getting used to them, they were sort of cute.

As a cheerer-upper I was as effective as a cup of weak tea. She shook her head. Moisture dampened her eyes – green eyes, tropic green, with long red lashes and arched by slim, slanting eyebrows the same glorious color as her hair.

"I can't tell you about it. I can't tell you anything unless I'll be sure you'll take the case. It's too private."

"You can tell me what's involved. Whether it's legal or not. Do I have to heist anyone? Steal anything?"

"No. You just have to follow a man. Investigate him. Find out everything you can about his past – and present."

"Well, that sounds as though it might be possible," I said, still cheerful. "But the key question is ... why? Is he a boy-friend or a husband you want to get the goods on?"

She shook her head. The red hair tossed about her shoulders like breakers playing with the shoreline on a breezy day.

"Is it a business deal – is he the executor of your father's millions, with embezzlement deep in his kind old eyes?"

"No."

"I don't get it. But if it's legit, I'll probably do it for you. As a personal favor." I let my hand rest briefly on hers, on the bar. It was a cool, slender hand. She took it quickly away and put it back in her purse, feeling for the money.

"It doesn't have to be as personal as all that," she said. But at last she was smiling again. The bands made straight, clean lines just below her smoothly crimson upper lip. I wondered idly how they would feel to the tip of an exploring tongue. It was only a thought.

She took the thousand dollars and wadded it into my breast pocket behind my dress handkerchief. "Now you're working for me," she said gaily.

I sighed. Maybe I was being sucked in. I always seemed to end up with 'sucker' printed on me in red poster paint when I got outside my own quiet, respectable league.

"I want you to find my father," she told me. "I don't know who he is."

So that was it. There was bound to be something illegitimate somewhere.

"Fine," I said. Somewhat bitterly. "Have you any twenty-year-old pictures of him I could study?"

"No," she smiled. "But it won't be as difficult as you think." She reached in the purse again and came out with an envelope. She gave it to me.

The envelope contained an airplane ticket for one Russell Teed. That was me. One-way, New York to Montreal, on North Coastal Airways, eleven p.m. the same evening. Fourteen hours from now I had to head back to Montreal. It seemed a little pointless. I said so. "This all seems a little pointless," I said.

The red eyebrows lifted.

"Why have me shoehorn myself into a roomette, bounce all the way down here and brave the wild bulls' stampede – the morning commuters' rush – just so you could send me right back?"

"Oh, you don't understand. This is the only chance you have to identify my father. He's going to be on that plane tonight. So you'll have at least one chance in fifteen of finding him right away. After he gets back to Montreal, the odds would be more like one in a million."

"You don't know who he is," I said carefully. "You've never known him. But he's going to be on that plane. All right, I'll admit I'm licked. I don't get any of it. Give."

"Will you take the case?"

"I suppose so," I grumbled.

She drew a deep breath. She paused. "First, I'll need a drink," she said. "Get me a ..."

"A whiskey sour?" I asked. I asked in a good loud voice so the bartender would hear.

"That would be just right." She smiled.

The bands were bright and clean and shining. I liked them. I wouldn't want her to be any other way. I was near the bottom of my Scotch and milk. By the time I'd finished the second, I would be wedded to those bands for life. I'd adore them. I could imagine being unable to do without them; or anyhow, unable to do without the particular model that came equipped with them.

She was lovely. I didn't know anything about her, except she'd misplaced her father. But then, how much do you ever know about anyone?

The bartender came. I could afford to gloat. "A whiskey sour, please," I said. "Along with another Scotch and milk."

"The story ..." she began, seriously.

"Wait." The mood was too good to spoil just now. "We'll go sit at a table. By the way, what do I call you?"

"Ann."

"Ann ... ?"

"That will be enough."

"Sorry. In my business I have to keep records."

"Ann ... Wedgewood," she said. The bands gave her speech just the smallest suggestion of an intriguing lisp.

"Sure it's not Ann Spode? Never mind. It'll do for now." I led her to a table.

The bartender brought the drinks. I gave him the wide, triumphant grin. "I hope you charged up the sour as a milk."

He took it well. "I guess we're even," he said.

Things were beginning to improve.

Scene Two

IT WAS THE OLD STORY, played straight with no twists. The characters were wealthier than usual, but it was the same old sad song.

About thirty years ago there lived in Westmount a girl who was called, in the story, Margaret. Westmount is the part of Montreal where the people who run the English side of their city do their sleeping. You wouldn't call it a dormitory of Montreal, but you might say it was the residential hotel.

Margaret's father was president of a chartered bank. Her mother was a woman fitted to be the wife of such a man. Margaret herself was lovely, gay, unspoiled. Chances were, I'd say ten to one, she had red hair.

Two blocks over and one block down lived a handsome, gay, and unspoiled youth. He met Margaret at a country club dance. She was eighteen at the time, and he twenty-two and doing as well as might be expected in his father's business.

They fell in love and wanted to get married. There were two lines of parental objection. First, from both families they got the line that they were too young. Then Margaret's family brought in a less creditable angle. Altitude means an awful lot in Westmount. They didn't want to be snobbish, but – well, after all the boy did live lower down the hill.

So they didn't get married. But – and this, though it seems a long time ago to you and me, was just at the shank of the flaming twenties – Margaret, nice girl though she was, discovered she was going to have a baby. Discovered it too late, being a shy, naive girl, for marriage even to be talked of.

Then, or so I judged from the way the story was told, Margaret's parents behaved remarkably well. They took part of the blame on their own shoulders. They arranged for her to go away and have the baby quietly, and no one was ever to know. And they did it all kindly, not heaping her with shame.

Margaret's baby was a girl. It was adopted, but the adoption arrangements then were not as strict as they now are. Margaret knew who had taken her baby. She could even make the long trip, occasionally, in secret, to see her child. Later she married. Her disposition was too sunny and her popularity too great to let the Great Mistake tear up her life. She married very well, into a circle of Westmount even higher than her own. She had other children, but she never forgot her first baby.

She had independent means, of course, after her parents died. She supported the child. Later, she made regular trips to see her, buy her clothes, influence the way she developed and grew. The child's foster parents were modest, poor; Margaret was the biggest influence on her life. She was quite young when she knew Margaret was her real mother.

Margaret sent her to Bryn Mawr, and after she had graduated helped her find a job in New York. That brought the story up-to-date.

Some of the clichés in the tale are mine, and some are Ann's, the way she told it. Margaret was Ann's mother.

The story took a long time to tell. We were old friends by the time it was told. I'd told my life story somewhere in the middle. The long, oval Commodore bar was filling up now for the pre-lunch cocktail, and getting noisy. It was still a nice bar, dim and cool and full of gleaming old mahogany. We sat at our little table within calling distance of our bartender, with an ashtray full of butts and two half-drunk whiskey sours – I'd gone off the milk train too.

"There are still some things I'll have to know," I said. Not demandingly, because we were friends.

"Of course," she said, with the little lisp, the lisp that went with the bands. I still noticed it; I hadn't gotten used to it, and it still intrigued me. Like the bands themselves.

"After all these years, why do you suddenly have to know all about your father?"

"Margaret came to New York to see me yesterday. She didn't mean to tell me anything, but she was in such a terrible stew that I wormed it out of her. After a very long time, my father had been in touch with her. He wanted to see her. She had come to New York to meet him – he still lives in Montreal, too, but they thought it wiser not to attempt to meet there."

"And – what? A revival of love? Or was it blackmail?"

"In a very refined way. Nothing so crude as money."

Quietly, my hand went to my breast pocket and caressed her thousand dollars. But I didn't say anything.

She went on quietly, "For some reason, my father is interested in the business Margaret's husband owns. He wanted to know some secrets. He was sure Margaret could find them out. Otherwise, he would tell my whole story. Not just to Margaret's husband, but publicly. Well. You know Westmount."

"It could be embarrassing," I admitted. "I begin to see what you want from me. I'm to investigate your father from stem to gudgeon. I pick up a few filthy episodes from his past or present. Then we do a little counter-blackmail."

"Do you think it would work?"

"It might. From the type of racket he's pulling on your mother, he can't be too clean a character. But first I have to find him."

"He'll be on the plane tonight."

"Have him wear a white carnation, will you? Look, this is silly as hell. Work on Margaret and get his name."

"She hasn't told anyone in almost thirty years. And anyone else who might know his identity is dead. She swears she'll keep the secret forever. That's why I telephoned you, last night. That's why I made you come down here."

"I'm sort of glad I did," I told her. The case sounded as though it wouldn't get me in too much trouble, but I wasn't thinking of that.

She colored. She knew what I meant. She smiled, and I saw her bands one last time, and she was gone to have lunch with her mother – Margaret – who remained unidentified beyond that, despite my best persuading.

She left me with an afternoon and evening to kill alone. In New York, that's not too desperate a position to be in.

Scene Three

ON SUNDAY NIGHT, at ten p.m., I had emerged from a taxi in front of Windsor Station in Montreal and walked into the station. It was now ten p.m. Monday, and I hadn't been in the open air since.

The train had deposited me in Grand Central. And from Grand Central, without getting your feet wet on a rainy day, you could go anywhere I wanted to go that day in New York. I had lunch in the Commodore Bar. After a while I sauntered across the concourse of Grand Central, through about four tunnels, and into the Men's Bar of the Roosevelt. When I got tired of the Men's Bar I tried the Roughrider Room. And then, when it was late enough and because the thousand dollars was burning a hole in my pocket, I went into the Grille and had dinner and listened to Guy Lombardo.

I guess it's a sign of age. There was a time when I scorned anything but Benny Goodman. Now Lombardo sends me. As far as I want to go that way.

I claimed my Gladstone, found my way back to Grand Central, drew my last deep breath of ventilation and emerged into the Forty-second Street air. It shocked me. It was raining harder than the day they floated the Ark. I got soaked dashing across the street to the Airlines Terminal.

All the way from New York to LaGuardia, the storm got worse. Twice the wind nearly blew the bus off the road. It could have done, and left me happy. I thought of flying through the stuff. I felt the milk in the Scotch in my stomach start to curdle.

The bus stopped near the line of little sheds they use for waiting rooms at the edge of LaGuardia Field. I got out and ran for the nearest doorway. It was blowing like a bad night on the North Atlantic and the rain was sneering and snapping around, making liars out of people who advertised their goods as waterproof. I crashed through the door of the building. I stopped in front of a counter labeled North Coastal Airways and tilted my head forward. The water from my hat brim drained to the floor and made a small puddle.

There were eight people sitting or standing around the little waiting room. The standing ones were nervous. They squinted from slitted eyes out along the shining asphalt ribbons of the landing strips. They were scared by the mere idea of flying on a night like this. You could see how frightened they were by the fascinated way they watched the runways, jerking their heads to inspect any light that moved.

Behind the counter, a thin clerk with rumpled black hair and practiced fingers was playing some private kind of solitaire with a pile of passenger checks. He dealt them out into five piles, stacked the piles, riffled them and dealt them out again to reverse the order. Then he looked up and said, "Yes, Sir?" in a voice that was a little tired of calling people 'Sir' at this time of night.

"Teed," I told him. "Flight 93 to Montreal. Does she fly?"

I hoped to God he'd say no.

"Yes, Sir." He fanned the checks, selected one and slapped it in front of him. He palmed a pencil and chanted the routine question: "Will you be using our limousine service from the airport into Montreal?"

"What time does the flight arrive?"

"Twelve-forty a.m."

"My chauffeur hates to drive after midnight," I said moodily. "I guess I'll have to take the limousine."

The clerk entered a checkmark on my card with a

baroque flourish. "Tch, tch," he said sympathetically. "No night chauffeur?"

"Not any more. Market's been off."

The clerk craned his neck to look past my shoulder into the far corner of the room. "Cedric Kelloway's just over there," he said. "Perhaps he'd let you drive into Montreal with him. Would you care to ask him, or shall I?"

I shook my head. "No, don't. Cedric and I aren't speaking since he got the senatorship I was promised."

Ah, what wit! Anything to take my mind off my stomach.

"Twelve million dollars, belted into a wet trench coat," the clerk said enviously. "Not often you can see that. Aren't you interested?"

I hadn't turned my head. "No," I said bitterly. Maybe he was my man. Maybe he was why I had to get up into this tortured air. "If you had twelve million iron men," I asked, "would you fly on a night like this?"

"He probably wants to get to the office on time tomorrow to be a good example to all the little clerks."

"Are you sure this flight will go out?"

"Yeah. Don't be nervous. It's a lot calmer upstairs. Besides, we haven't lost a passenger in six years on this run."

That got my dudgeon all riled up. "I've flown through weather like this with the cockpit covers off," I growled. "But I'll tell you a sad story. I sat down in the middle of the Atlantic once on a rubber raft for three days. Now the walls of my stomach try to clap hands when I go around a corner fast on a bicycle."

He looked at me sadly. "Fly-boy?" he asked. "R.C.A.F.?"

I shook my head. "Army. I got flown around the pond a lot."

"Army? I was Army. I hate fliers. Listen," he said confidentially. He leaned over the counter. "I can't leave here, but go through the door beside the counter and into the first office. Look in the bottom drawer. Afterward, you'll be sicker when you're sick. But you won't mind."

"Your soul is white," I said. I got out my wallet and gave him a card. "Anything I can ever do," I said. "Anything."

It was Seagram's V.O. When I came back to the room I felt stronger. The pilot could play hopscotch with the clouds if he wanted to. I tipped my hat solemnly to the clerk and took a seat where I could watch Kelloway.

Senator Cedric Kelloway, that is.

He was a neat little man. The hair of his head was white and sparse – there was just enough to make his pink scalp decent. Each individual hair was brushed straight. He had small white teeth arranged in two neat, even rows and he moved his lips tidily back and forth across them when he talked. His features were neat – pale blue eyes set straight under his Rinso-white eyebrows, a small-scale traditional nose, a chin laid out by an experienced draughtsman with the angles matched to thirty-second tolerances. God had been in a fussy mood the day he was engineered.

His clothes were almost too neat. He wore a suit that had cost $250 and two tailors' lives on Beaver Hall Hill; it was a nice executive grey. His shirt was individually hand-tailored so discreetly you hardly noticed it was a custom job. He had consulted a leading Canadian artist and two design specialists before picking out his tie. His shoes were the kind that are too good to polish; a man came in every morning to breathe on them and flick the dust specks away with a chamois.

Kelloway had lived a neat life, too. He had arranged to be born in the upper reaches of Westmount, of a father who had gone out some years before that and found five or six good base metal mines. Cedric had parlayed this into a nicely-organized empire – nothing gaudy, only the largest in Canada. Then he developed a political conscience. Getting appointed Senator was about as hard for him as coming first in the class when your father has paid off the mortgage on the school.

He was about five feet three and more men were afraid of him than of Yvon Robert.

He was neat, all right. But there might be one untied thing about his life – one untied string. He was about the right age.

He could be Ann's father.

Before I went sinking my teeth into conclusions like, one might say, a bulldog sinks his teeth into glutei maximi, I looked around at the other candidates present.

First, the man with Kelloway. Kelloway seemed to be dictating memos. He would purse his lips and say something. The man with him would nod solemnly, and then put his head back and stare at the ceiling and mesmerize it into his memory, another item on the mental checklist. The character was a great hulking gorilla with enough black hair to upholster a Ford coupe. He looked as though Kelloway owned a controlling interest in his soul and had been talking of throwing out the current management. He was of no further interest to me as a prospect, because he was way too young.

There were two others you could eliminate. They were both among the nervous standees. The first was short with a small black moustache, long hair and very high-waisted pants. He might be French-Canadian. He was too young. The second was a colored man in a clerical collar. He was only the second colored airplane passenger I'd ever seen. He was big, a bit soft, and dark as the heart of Africa at night. He was so frightened he shook every time the wind howled.

Two women were waiting for the plane. One very, very ugly girl. One grey-haired old Helen Hokinson club matron, so tired she could barely keep her eyes open.

Sitting between them was a possibility. He was a middle-aged man with a sad, droopy face and a glazed, hangover look in his eyes as though he'd started drinking too early in the afternoon and his stomach had gone bad on him. It was hard to imagine him as a Lothario, even thirty years before, but anything is possible.

There was also a man best described as a cheap imitation of the Senator. He was constructed to a larger scale, and much less carefully. His hair was plentiful and blue-white, and his eyebrows were jet black. It gave him a stagey look; he should have used the same blue rinse on both. But maybe he wanted to look stagey. He seemed to enjoy putting on an act. Right then he was promoting himself a pleasant plane ride, talking with the girl beside him. He had his dial set to Charm, and he was putting it out like a college president working on the Wealthiest Alumnus.

The girl he was promoting was a showgirl. Showgirl, from the crown of her professional bleach job to the tips of her gilded pumps. I'd seen her somewhere, maybe in a Montreal nightclub, and I couldn't remember much more than that. I seemed to recall she was a singer, one of the type that sings with the expression in the body instead of in the voice. That didn't give me much of a lead for singling her out.

The blue-haired old stager was telling her something amusing. She kept nodding her head and smiling. On a nice girl it would have been a mischievous smile. On her it was mischievous like a Borgia in the butler's pantry.

After quite a bit of this she nodded, still smiling. She got up and volupted to the end of the room where Kelloway and his black-haired oversize yes-boy were sitting. I heard

her say to the yes-boy, "Hello, Donald." She said it famil-
iarly. The rest I lost. She was telling him something and
he was trying to look like she was the village drunk from
the old hometown, someone you couldn't brush right off
but would like to see drop discreetly dead. The Senator
was registering no expression and you couldn't even be
sure he saw her.

Showgirl was saying something serious to yes-boy, if
you went by her expression. While she talked she nodded
toward her blue-haired boyfriend, as though maybe she
was repeating something he'd told her. Then she turned
and looked across the room and the yes-boy followed her
eyes. It was a little hard to tell who they inspected. I guessed
at either the sleepy old matron or the Negro minister. After
that, she went back to her own seat. She left the yes-boy a
nervous wreck. He squirmed in his chair. He didn't say
anything to Kelloway, probably because it wasn't protocol
for him to speak without being bespoken, but he waited
for the Senator to ask him something. The Senator, though,
wasn't in an asking mood. He was dreaming with his eyes
open, probably about 40% ore concentrates.

I went to the ticket counter. My friend and benefactor,
the clerk, was talking to a pilot. "Passenger list?" I asked
him quietly. He shoved me his pad.

The showgirl's name stuck out like a bowtie at a truck
drivers' convention. Lorette Toledo. She'd been singing
early in the summer at Lucio's, a clip joint on the Decarie
Sunset Strip. She sang smut songs. Some were funny and
some weren't, but they dragged in a certain class of business. I remember they held her there so long I gave up
going to the place.

No wonder Kelloway's boy had been unhappy to see
her.

Unless somebody arrived later to board the plane, I

only had three men who could be Ann's father: the Senator, the hangover St. Bernard type, and the man with blue hair. I took myself a running jump at eliminating one. I sallied at the showgirl and her friend.

"Miss Toledo," I mouthed. As close to a coo as I could make it.

She looked up with a mixture of pleased surprise and complete cold freeze. The expression could slide either way, depending on whether I was a reporter or a process server.

"I saw you here and recognized you and I saw you, oh, about twenty times at Lucio's this summer," I gabbled. "And I couldn't – I hope you don't mind – I just couldn't miss this opportunity to speak to you."

I got my handkerchief out of my pocket and held it concealed in my hand, ready in case I gagged if I had to do any more of this.

She flashed a row of expensive white porcelain. She said, "Why, you're so kind. Of course I'm glad to talk to an admirer." The voice was low and husky and supposed to be sexy. She'd got it from years of yelling filthy names after men who left her room without paying.

"Are you coming back to Montreal?"

"Yes, thanks to people like you. Loyal, loyal people. I'll be singing at Lucio's as long as you want me to stay."

"Ah," I said. It was a great awed, wondering sigh. "I'll be there to hear you tomorrow night."

"And I'll sing a song especially for you. What one do you like? The Lewd Horseman?"

"That one's just dandy," I said. "And how about your uncle, here? Is he your accompanist?"

She hadn't known the blue-haired daddy long enough to take that one for what it was worth. She smiled. She said, "Why, no, Mr. Scarper here isn't in the business any more. But he was just telling me how he used to emcee shows in the big clubs in Chicago."

I looked at Mr. Scarper. Mr. Blue-hair Scarper. I grinned ingratiatingly. "You come from Chicago, Mr. Scarper?" I asked pleasantly.

"Why, yes, I used to," he said.

You couldn't prove it by his voice. But the voice didn't sound as though it ever came from Westmount either.

The clerk clicked on his PA mike just then and began the usual routine about all passengers verifying their space before boarding. That gave me an out and I left them. I figured I hated it pared down to two: old dogface, and the Senator.

I could have flipped a coin, but I didn't. I chose the obvious. Why was there so much secrecy about this business? Why wouldn't Margaret give Ann her father's name? Probably because he was some very high-publicity-value type. Probably, by elimination, because he was Senator Cedric Kelloway.

The clerk's voice came over the PA system again; the low-fidelity speaker gave his voice a hoarse, gravelly rasp. "Passengers for Flight 93, passengers for Flight 93," he said. "Flight 93 now loading at gate number two. No smoking beyond the barrier."

The senator was surprisingly fast on his feet. He was the first one to the gate. The first one, after me. I stood aside to let him past. His yes-boy tried to squeeze through with him but I cut in between. The boy and I went through the doorway together without jamming, but only because I've never played football. We paced each other across the wet strip to the plane, following Kelloway. Then I inched ahead. I was on the passenger stairway right behind the Senator. I heard the boy curse under his breath.

I followed the Senator up the aisle. The plane was a

DC-3 with double seats on the left, singles on the right.

I expected him to sit in a double, leaving space for yes-boy beside him, which I would grab. But he fooled me. Maybe he was tired of talking, or perhaps he liked the feeling of sitting next to the emergency door. He sat in a single. I sat down in the double seat across the aisle from the Senator, in the chair next to the aisle. Yes-boy came along and stood beside me, waiting for me to move in and make him some room. I didn't look at him, and I didn't move. He stood there for a minute trying to make up his mind to speak. Then he remembered how much the Senator liked scenes. He lurched back and sat down behind me.

The plane was only half-full and no one came to sit with him. Two people went on up the aisle and passed me – the very ugly girl and the sleepy matron, who stumbled twice before she fell into a seat. The rest sat somewhere behind. The gusty rain splatted the aluminum skin of the fuselage in patterns, like birdshot. We taxied cross-wind out to the end of the runway and the wind blasted the plane irregularly, bumping it into little skids and swaying the wings. I began to remember my stomach.

But then we got down to the end of the runway, revved up and took off against the wind almost effortlessly. We drifted easily across Manhattan. The stewardess turned off the sign that kept passengers from smoking.

I noticed she left burning the one that said, 'Fasten Your Safety Belts.'

The Reverend Negro was the first to get sick. He whooped when he was being sick, in a kind of hopeless moan. It was not encouraging to anyone trying to face the situation calmly.

The plane was about an hour out of LaGuardia. There hadn't been any bumps, just plain rough weather. The wind was quartering across from behind, feathering the propellers so the whole plane shook with their rough vibration and the cabin filled up with the uneven grinding of the motors. Every minute or so the wind would sneak up from behind and kick the plane in the undercarriage. It would bounce forward indignantly like a goosed dowager and then settle back grumbling to a steady course.

I hadn't got sick yet, but only because I was concentrating on setting up and opening with the Senator. Kelloway was doing fine. His pastel pink little puss had not done any fading. Obviously he wasn't planning to do anything as earthy as retch. He felt so well, in fact, that he pulled out a small, neat pipe and delicately filled it. He lit up, and the smoke that came my way smelled expensive as a bad night at Monte Carlo. I wasn't the only one to smell the smoke. The stewardess came up and hove to between the Senator and me.

"Sorry, sir," she said pleasantly. "No pipe smoking."

The Senator pointed to the front of the cabin. "The No Smoking sign isn't lighted." He wasn't ornery about it. He was a lot pleasanter than I'd expected him to be.

The stewardess shook his head. "Only cigarettes permitted. I'm sorry. The ventilation on DC-3's isn't enough to carry away pipe smoke. And it's a pretty rough trip."

Then she went away. She would go back down the aisle to her galley and get a little packet of complimentary cigarettes and bring them to him. But I knew a chance when I saw one. I hauled the State Express pack out of my pocket and bellowed across the aisle, "Pardon me. But may I offer you a smoke?"

He smiled and nodded and took one.

"Too bad about the pipe," I said.

He shrugged. "I'm used to that. Sometimes I can get

away with it on a plane. But I suppose she doesn't want any more sick. Have you heard the way that great black jellied ox back there is whooping?"

I swallowed hard and nodded.

He went on, with sadistic detachment, "I've been looking back. I see a lot of green faces. The young lady with blonde hair is going to be sick any instant. I wouldn't be surprised if everyone except the crew is sick, this trip. The crew, and me. I'm never airsick." He smiled at me cruelly. "How do you feel?"

I tried to smile back at him, but I didn't have a smile left in me.

A little later, I didn't have anything left in me. It took about ten minutes to lose my dinner, but in five minutes more I was through with lunch and breakfast – I was well into the rhythm of the business by then. After that I spent some time losing meals I'd forgotten eating.

I came slowly back to life. My mouth tasted like something that needed flushing down a toilet. My eyes watered and my ears didn't hear. I lit a cigarette, and it tasted liked chopped alfalfa.

I had one consolation. Everybody else in the cabin, with the exception of the stewardess and the Senator, was concentrated on trying to hit the inside of a paper cup.

As for the Senator, even that old hyena's stomach couldn't take a plane trip like this one. He was out cold. The color had faded from his smooth pink face, leaving it white with a grey overcast. He was slumped down in his seat, head back and mouth slightly open.

Then I saw the mark on his forehead.

Scene Four

I UNDID MY SAFETY BELT and moved carefully into the aisle. Just then the right wing tip of the DC-3 hit an air draft no harder than granite, spun the plane around and pasted me back into my seat. It was the kind of night witches get blown off their broomsticks. I tried again. I grabbed the arm of the Senator's chair before I let go my own. This time I made it.

The cabin was full of ragged vibrating noise. I bent down to Kelloway's ear and shouted, "Senator!" No answer. I looked at the mark. It was a red curve, perhaps half an inch wide and two inches long, on the side of his head just behind the temple. The only reason I could see it was because the Senator's hair was so thin and colorless. It was beginning to darken, like a bruise.

There was no pulse at the wrist. I pulled away his suit coat and felt for his heart. It told me he wasn't dead. I jammed my finger on the call button for the stewardess.

I had to wait. The stewardess was a busy girl. She was helping people be sick. Most of them didn't need much help.

I bent back over Kelloway. He hadn't stirred but his heart was still going, hesitantly. I looked up again and the stewardess was approaching with two paper cartons at the ready – lids off and all set to be used. They were the round cardboard cans that airlines put under the seat and any passenger who is fast on the draw can retch into one. The stewardess had an extra supply, and assumed from recent experience that was what we wanted.

I hadn't paid enough attention to this stewardess before. Now even with the Senator conking off I took time out to appreciate her. She was black Irish, with long hair under her little hat, smooth and shining as black satin. The eyes were hazel, more the color of the Pacific than of the Atlantic, and deeper than either. The nose was low-bridged and symmetrical, the chin a little too long and too broad – a chin with more character than a whole synod of bishops. She wore lipstick with more black than red in it, and I liked her lower lip. I liked her upper lip too. Her uniform did a fair job of concealing her figure, but she wasn't deformed. She would be worth waiting two hours for in a bar. Maybe even on a street corner.

I looked to the front of the cabin, and her name was on the crew list. Stewardess, M. Malone. "Miss Malone," I said, "meet Senator Kelloway. He's been careless. Something has whonked him on the noggin."

She frowned concernedly. She had to be a nurse to have this job, but she wasn't the professional hack with the surgical steel manner. "Did he try to leave his seat, and fall in the aisle?" she asked. She talked like something out of Finian's Rainbow, but she was trying to take the accent off, not put it on.

"I didn't see what he did. But his safety belt's clasped."

"It must have happened a few moments ago. He's in deep shock." She went efficiently to work, loosening his collar, pulling a blanket down from the overhead rack to cover him.

I didn't tell her he was dying.

I left her and swayed up the aisle to the pilot's cabin. I opened the door. The squeaky rattle of the radio signals fluttered in my ears. I went past the luggage compartment and squatted on the runway behind the crew's seats. It was a DC-3, meaning the space was crowded.

The captain said without looking around, "How are things, Maida? Got time to bring me some coffee?"

So her name was Maida. Maida Malone.

I said, "It isn't Maida, and I want to talk to you."

He did look around then, and he got mad. "On a night like tonight, we got to have a sleepwalker aboard," he yapped. "Get out. You know passengers aren't allowed in here."

He was more put out than he might have been other times, because the co-pilot was sick. The co-pilot's face was grey-green and he was leaning back in his seat with his eyes shut and his mouth clamped tight, trying to forget he's ever seen a Link Trainer.

I surveyed him. "Don't worry, he doesn't shake my morale," I told the captain. "Sorry I broke in. But there's trouble in the cabin. A man's dying."

He eyed me like the president of the corporation receiving a complaint from the elevator starter. "Okay," he said. "Put it all down in writing and send it in by the stewardess. I'll work it over after I've finished playing with this tailwind."

"Okay, brush me off. You don't have to pay me attention. The guy is only Senator Kelloway."

The plane ran into a small part of the universe where the air had been moved to the next precinct, and dropped into the vacuum like a skier going down a hill to the tavern at the bottom.

The captain pulled the wheel with one hand and shoved my head out of his lap with the other.

"Next time I'll fix it so you leave by the windscreen," he said. "Now will you go back and tie yourself down?"

"Do you want to hear this?"

"How do you know it's Kelloway? And how do you know he's dying?

"I know it's Kelloway because I've seen him before. And I've seen people dying before. In large numbers, between 1939 and 1945."

"What happened to him?"

"He got hit on the head."

"How? Something break loose and fall on him?"

"I don't know. I was sick. Everybody in the cabin is sick, except Maida. I doubt if anyone can tell what hit him. Maybe he was slugged."

"It's a possibility," the captain agreed. "Is he really going to cash in? Can't Maida do anything for him?"

I shook my head. "He's got a cracked skull. You might tell them to have an ambulance meet us at Dorval, but I think he's had the course."

"Okay, okay. What else do you want me to do?"

"Cops."

"Look, brother, this is Senator Kelloway. I don't just go yelling for cops at random. Maybe he wouldn't like the publicity."

"He won't be kicking."

"Maybe Mrs. Kelloway would."

"Why? She isn't on the plane. She didn't knock him off."

"You think somebody did?"

"It would be awful hard for him to fall on his face while his safety belt was fastened."

"Huh. I see what you mean," he growled.

"Are you going to do something?"

"Notify Dorval."

"And what will they do?"

"Nothing I don't tell them to. There's only a few flunkies in our office this time of night."

"We need cops. Grade A homogenized cops. Better tell Dorval to call R.C.M.P. headquarters in Montreal. Ask for Inspector Dorset, he's their night man. Say Kelloway has been seriously injured on this plane, maybe dying, maybe foul play. Dorset'll do something."

The captain thought it over. "The Mounties would keep quiet if there was really nothing wrong, wouldn't they?"

"Sure. And I've got a split lip. It hurts me to talk."

"And who are you?"

"Russell Teed. I come from Montreal. Private op. You can tell Dorset I found the injured man, if you want to. He knows me."

"Okay," the captain said. I started back. "And tell Maida to bring me some coffee," he called after me.

Maida Malone was bending over the Senator. The plane lurched on and she swayed back and forth, close to his face, away, close. Something like the way you might play with a baby, pushing your face up close to make him laugh, then ducking away again. Only the Senator wasn't laughing.

Maida was using one hand to brace herself. She held Kelloway's wrist with the other, and his hand flapped over and over and over again, aimlessly, loosely, with the motion of the plane.

She looked up at me, and her expression bothered me. She wasn't tough enough for a nurse. She had been crying. "He's dead," she said. "There wasn't anything I could do. He's dead."

I looked at my watch. It was 12:20 a.m. and the plane was due at Dorval at 12:40. I didn't even know whether he'd died over Canada or the United States. The R.C.M.P. could worry about that.

I wouldn't meet her eyes. Still looking at my watch I said, "You'd better tell the captain. And he wants a cup of coffee." Maida went uncertainly back toward her galley.

The Senator made a frail little corpse. The mortician was going to have to color him up well to make him look good. He was as grey as his suit. The contusion beside his temple had turned an ugly purple color.

He was always so neat. It seemed too bad to leave him there all rumpled up. I braced myself and lifted his shoulders, straightening him in the seat. I pulled back the blanket and tightened his safety belt to hold him there. His eyes were closed. I closed his mouth.

I took his small, veined hands to fold them in his lap. One hung loosely by his side. The right hand seemed stuck down at the side of the seat between his body and the upholstery. I pulled it up. With it came a small leather-covered loose-leaf book – a pocket memo book.

The book came easily out of his hand. I dropped it in my side pocket.

Maida Malone passed in the aisle, with coffee on a tray. She motioned with her head. "That man across the aisle – one seat back. He told me he was traveling with Senator Kelloway."

I nodded. "I know."

"Would you please tell him? I didn't have time to call him, and he's been sick."

"What's his name?"

"Willcot," she said. "Donald Willcot."

Willcot, the yes-boy. I looked at him.

Kelloway must have chosen him for contrast. He was big enough to make about 3.4 Kelloways. He had a football player's shoulders and a hockey player's thighs, and his feet were about size 15. He was enveloped in a raincoat no bigger than a 6-man Army bell-tent, and his thick black hair was tousled. His face was square and blue as a slate roof. His chin had no point; it had corners.

Willcot had been sick, probably with violence to match his physical size. There were splashes. He was resting, head back, eyes closed. He winced every time the plane bounced. He likely thought he wouldn't last as far as Dorval.

I tapped his shoulder. He opened his eyes slowly and looked at me. When he saw who it was, his face darkened and he stuck his underslung jaw out a little further.

Truculent would be a very mild word for Mr. Donald Willcot just then.

"I'd like to talk to you a minute," I said.

"Why?"

"I have something," I said patiently, "that I would like to talk about."

"You've something to explain first. That horsing around when we got on the plane."

"I'll explain it," I said. He was sitting in the aisle half off his double seat. I squeezed past him and sat down in the seat next the window. I was putting myself in a vulnerable position, but I probably knew more jiu-jitsu than he did.

The jiu-jitsu was something I was going to need, and need badly, if he started suspecting the story I was going to tell him.

"My name is MacArnold," I said. "I'm a reporter for the Montreal *Citizen*. I was in New York covering the United Nations session at Lake Success when I got a wire to catch this plane and talk to the Senator."

"What about?"

"You tell me. Whatever he came to New York for, I guess."

"So?"

"I was playing it quietly. The Senator's never talked to me, so he wouldn't recognize me as a newsman. I know how he likes reporters, so I didn't just come up to him with my pencil and notebook out. I fixed it to sit next to him in the plane."

"You newsmen," he said, with feeling, "are a low bunch of filthy bastards."

"Oh, not all of us. I'm worse than most."

"White of you to admit it," he said, but he didn't mean to flatter me. "Well, I thought you were something as bad. I thought you must be a bond salesman trying to get his ear. I was watching you."

"Until you got sick."

"That's right, I got sick," Willcot said in a hard voice. He didn't like being reminded.

"It's a hell of a night to fly. Why didn't he postpone his trip until tomorrow?"

"Because he wanted to come back tonight," Willcot said carefully. "And besides, he's never sick on planes."

"Were you in New York long?"

"Ask him," Willcot grated. "Or have you talked to him already and been brushed off?"

"No chance. I waited careful-like to get a good opening with him. I waited too long. I got sick."

Willcot smiled. It reminded me of a rock cracking open.

I stuck a wedge in the crack before it could close up again. "Sure, newsmen are bastards. Sometimes," I said sheepishly. "But you have to get beer-money somehow. It's a job."

"I know what you mean," he assured me.

"You like yours?"

"The old guy's not bad."

"What are you, his private secretary? You don't look the type."

"I'm not. It was all a big mistake, I was working for one of his mines up north – engineer. We got called into conference with him in Montreal, and I shot my mouth off too much, I guess. I told him I'd stake my reputation on the payoff if he opened up a new ore body I'd staked out. I talked him into it. Maybe I was trying to play up to him – I don't know. I had my eye on the mine manager's job there. I should sink so low. After the ore body was proved out, this is what it got me."

I looked at him. He would have made a good hockey goalie – with very little padding and no stick. "Did he want a secretary or a bodyguard?" I wondered.

"Bodyguard," he told me, deadpan.

"Why?"

"To keep reporters away. Anything else I can tell you?"

"Anything else you *will* tell me?"

"No," he said definitely.

"I started out to tell you something, really. Something about him. Sorry I got sidetracked."

"You can't tell me anything about him."

I didn't argue. I pointed to Kelloway.

Willcot leaned forward and looked. "Oh, asleep, eh? Hey, what the hell? He's got the blanket right up over his head."

"He had an accident," I said. "Sorry. He isn't asleep. He's dead."

Willcot kept on looking at him for about a full minute. Then he turned slowly back to me. A heavy flush colored his face. "I believe you," he whispered. It wasn't shock that had softened his voice; he was raging mad.

"I believe you," he rasped again, "but I wish I hadn't listened to anything else you said. What have you been trying to do, you cheap hack, build up a good story? Reactions of personal secretary to great man's death? Just a few paragraphs, background stuff you got from me, to pad out the column? I thought you were low with the first trick you pulled. But you aren't just low. You're something blind and colorless and slimy that lives on dead things in the bottom of a stagnant pond. If I thought there was one more like you in the world I'd kill myself."

Willcot got up and swayed in the aisle. His trenchcoat floated about him like a parachute. "Get away from here," he spat.

I got up slowly. I was as tall as he was, but about half his weight. It didn't worry me. He wasn't going to hit me because I was too low to hit. And there was nothing I could say to him.

It's a nice business I'm in. I beat up beautiful girls and seduce old women to get information. I even do things like this. I felt almost as low as he thought I was. It didn't matter that I'd probably saved his life.

The Senator, for my money, had not been just killed. He'd been murdered, by somebody on the plane. Taking the suspects in order, anybody would start out with Willcot. He was probably the only person on the plane who knew Kelloway personally. But, if I swung any weight with whoever investigated the case, they wouldn't pin him. Because he hadn't known Kelloway was dead when I started talking to him. He couldn't have known. Nobody can act that well.

Sometime, after things got to a later stage, maybe I could try to explain that to him. If I could ever get close enough to explain. Don't bring your boy up to be a detective.

So he didn't do it. So who did?

Maida was puttering around in her galley at the back of the cabin. "Hi," I said.

"Hello." Gravely.

"I wonder what could have hit the Senator. I can't figure it."

"Something hit him good and hard, the poor old man. His skull must have been fractured, for him to go so quickly."

"Couldn't have been anything falling on him?"

She wrinkled her clear white forehead. "No. Nothing goes on the overhead rack but blankets and pillows. Never anything heavier than a briefcase, just for this very reason. So people won't be struck. You said his safety belt was fastened. It was fastened when you first looked at him, after you saw he was ill?"

"That's right. He was trussed in solid as a payphone on a wall."

"You were in the best position to see what happened," she pointed out. "You were sitting opposite him."

"Yes, and I picked a fine time to be sick. I was gazing into a cardboard cup while somebody was socking Kelloway."

Her eyes widened, and she suddenly looked so frightened I wanted to take her in my arms and comfort her. Or at least, it looked for a few seconds as though I had a chance of getting away with it. "Oh! Is that what you think happened?" she whispered.

"You tell me what else happened to him."

"Then somebody ... "

"Did anyone walk down the aisle about that time?"

"I ... Everybody was sick then. I was so busy. Most of the passengers in the plane could have walked down the aisle, and I wouldn't have noticed. Or at least I wouldn't have remembered. I don't suppose the passengers will remember, either. Hardly one could lift his head."

"Think carefully," I said, "and tell me one thing. Were all the passengers sick?"

Her eyes moved down the cabin and checked them off one by one. Reading from the back of the cabin we had first the colored minister. Two seats in front of him, together, the blue-haired Scarper – on the outside – and Lorette Toledo. Across the aisle from them, old dog Tray with his mournful eyes. Up one, little moustache and

Donald Willcot. Then the body, and my empty seat. Farther front the ugly girl, and the matron.

Maida considered each one. When she was through she nodded her head. "They were all sick. You were the last one to go under. The Senator was the only one who didn't."

"Well, sick or not, one of them did it. The Senator didn't die of erysipelas."

"But – these people are all strangers. Who could have wanted to kill him?"

"Who? Why? How? I don't know. Except for the how, I can guess that. Otherwise, I hope Inspector Dorset has fun."

Scene Five

Inspector John Dorset, R.C.M.P., stood framed in the cabin doorway as the door opened. He fitted the door the way a cork fits a bottle. He was middle-aged and paunchy and it had been many long years since he sat on a horse.

He had an unexciting, almost unlined face, and he looked as though he might bumble a bit from time to time. A lock of brittle, dying grey hair dropped down below his water-soaked hat. His eyes looked water-soaked, too; they were very mild and quiet. He had an old, seamy scar down one cheek where a half-breed had pulled a knife on him once and he hadn't ducked fast enough.

I'd known him for a long time. His appearance was about as true to his nature as a gigolo's wardrobe is to his personal fortune. He had a mind like a Friden automatic calculator and the incident with the half-breed was the only one where he'd failed to move quickly, in thirty years of service.

I was waiting for him at the door. "Hi, Inspector. Congratulations," I said.

"Don't be flip, Mr. Teed," Dorset said calmly. "And please stand aside. I want to come in before anyone leaves the plane."

"And I want to come out. Seal the door with your signet ring and let the rest wait for a while."

"You can just sit down with the rest."

"I want to talk to you alone. It's my idea you're here."

"The Airline office called me," Dorset said.

"I asked them to." I lowered my voice. "There's been a murder done in here. One of the most important men in the country's been killed, and you're the avenging bloodhound. That's why I congratulated you. Aren't you going to thank me for bringing you in?"

"No," he said stolidly. "And now, go back and sit down. I'll get around to you."

I backed up a few feet. He came into the cabin. I said, "Okay, so I can't talk to you like that. I apologize. But I found him just after he got bashed, I'm the one that thinks it's murder, and I had the pilot call you. Give me five minutes with you – outside."

His pale eyes considered me. You could almost hear him thinking. Then he said, "Wait." He brushed past me and went to the Senator's body. Pulling back the blanket, he studied the dead man's face and head. Then he came back. He jerked his head toward the door, and we went out.

The weather wasn't much better than the New York weather had been. There was less wind but more rain. I have seen rain in Halifax that came down harder, but only a few times. Three R.C.M.P. constables in flat-brimmed khaki hats and long, flapping rubber coats like ponchos were grouped about the bottom of the landing staircase. There was a big ambulance drawn up beside the plane.

"We'll get soaked if we talk here," I pointed out.

"We can go sit in the ambulance."

"I need a drink. But the best thing you can get in this place is a cup of coffee. Let's go to the restaurant."

"Oh, no, Mr. Teed. I'm not going to leave those people cooped up in the plane while you lap coffee."

"I shouldn't tell you your business, but why not take them to the Customs waiting room? The constables can watch them there and one can stay with the plane."

He thought that one over for a second and decided there was nothing wrong with it. He gave orders to the constables and then, leaning against the wind and holding our hats, we ran to the terminal building.

The restaurant was really a lunch counter. It was a long room with a low coffee bar and low chairs instead of stools in front of the bar, so you could keep your feet on the ground and sit fairly comfortably.

I got coffee with no cream, refused the sugar and took a long drink while it was still steaming. I got out my cigarettes and gave one to Dorset and one to me and lit them. There was no one sitting near us.

Dorset said, "So Senator Kelloway is dead."

"Dead as your afternoon paper. His spirit left these familiar four dimensions just before 12:20 a.m."

"Couldn't you stick to simple phrases, like, 'He died at 12:20?'" Dorset grumbled mildly. "We might get along with it faster. Now, just what happened? What do you have to talk to me about?"

"About the way he died. I was sitting right across the aisle from him. We even exchanged a few words. Then, I suppose at around ten to twelve, I got sick. I wasn't alone – it was like a rough trip across the Bay of Fundy. Everybody was sick except the hostess."

I drained the coffee, put out the cigarette, and said, "When I could lift my head again I glanced at the Senator. He was out cold. I thought at first he'd been sick too. Then I saw that welt on the side of his head. I went over and listened to him tick, but he wasn't ticking so well. He was on his way out."

"While you were being sick," Dorset said, "he got up to go back to the lavatory, or to get a magazine from the rack up front. He fell and struck his head on something sharp, like the metal side of a seat or the metal step at the side of the aisle. He hauled himself back into his seat and passed out."

"Sure," I said, "only first he fastened himself in with his safety belt, tight as a Scotch pocket flap."

"He was that way when you found him?"

"He was."

"Huh," said Dorset. It meant he thought I might have something.

"So someone in there slugged him on the side of the head."

"Maybe, maybe not. You didn't see it happen."

"No, damn it."

"Well, assume you're right. Somebody approaches Kelloway and hits him on the side of the head. Now, that sounds sensible, doesn't it? Who would be that crazy? The killing might have been seen by anyone on the plane."

"No. The cabin lights were dim, the way they usually are on a night flight. And everybody was sick. No one was looking at anything but the inside of a paper can. Whoever did it waited until I was sick too."

"The stewardess might have seen him."

"She was busy as a short-order chef at lunchtime. The murderer just had to wait until she was at the other end of the cabin bending over a sick passenger."

"Yes, but look. If Kelloway was struck hard enough to kill him, it was done with something very solid and heavy. A blackjack, a revolver butt, perhaps a wrench. There must have been a weapon of some kind or other. And that would make it too risky. Even if the passengers were sick, one could easily look up. No, Mr. Teed. Senator Kelloway was an important man and it's a good thing you had me called, but I expect it was an accident. I think we'll find he slipped and fell. We can probably get some evidence of that by going over the plane carefully; the object he hit will be marked."

"How did his safety belt get fastened up again?"

"Let me tell you the way these head injuries act. When a man gets a blow on the head he'll black out for a few seconds, from the concussion. Then he comes to again. Later, if severe damage has been done, there'll be hemorrhage in the brain and he goes into a coma and perhaps dies. But there could easily have been time for Kelloway to get up, get back in his seat and fasten the belt."

"It's possible, provided one thing," I said.

"Yes?"

"Provided you don't find the weapon. Search the plane, the passengers – even me, if you want to. Empty the cans we were sick into. Open up the chemical can. Nothing got thrown off the plane on the flight, so the weapon must be in the cabin or on the person of a passenger. If you find a weapon, I'm right. If you don't, I'm wrong."

"If we find anything that even might have been the weapon, I'll consider he could have been murdered," Dorset agreed.

"Are you going to search them down to the skin?"

"Yes. Customs have a full staff on tonight – including a woman inspector. I'll explain to them what we're looking for and let them handle it. They're experts. I'm going to go over the plane myself."

"Do me now," I said. "I want to get out of here."

"I would think you'd stick around to see whether you're right or wrong."

"I have other things to do."

"There are certain things you won't do, unless you want me to lose my liking for you. Don't go talking to outside people. Don't tell the papers."

"I won't tell anyone it was murder," I said. "Not until we know. And when will we know?"

"After the search, I presume," he said mildly.

"I mean, what time?"

"Say three-thirty. I've got to interview each passenger,

and the crew, one by one. Just a preliminary interview, find out who they are and where I can locate them. Tell them to hold themselves ready for further questioning. And while their memories are fresh I can ask them if they remember anyone moving around in the aisle."

"You think I may be right," I accused him.

"I'm thorough," Dorset said. He wasn't boasting; it was just his statement of the way he did his job. "I'll be back in my office at three-thirty, or shortly afterward. Call me there and I'll tell you what happened. Or – no, you'd better come around. I might want to ask you something more."

"I know where the place is," I said.

"I hope you're wrong," he grunted. He was worried, and it rode heavily on his calm face. "I looked at the people on that plane, Teed. They weren't criminals. If this was murder, it wasn't done for any of the ordinary reasons – jealousy or hate or money. It wasn't just done by a thug. It was probably done by some God-fearing ordinary soul who couldn't let the Senator live. That would mean crawling all through the lives of those people on the plane, to find out why."

"The murder was unpremeditated," I said, "don't forget that."

"What do you mean?"

"The stormy night. The rough plane ride. The murderer wouldn't have dared, on a calm night."

"Mr. Teed," Dorset said chidingly, "Mr. Teed, be more exact in your language. Don't say, 'The murder was unpremeditated.' You don't mean that, you know. You mean ... the method of the murder was unpremeditated."

He stirred the last of his coffee, lifted the spoon out and stared gloomily at the half-melted sugar oozing back into the cup. He tossed off the coffee and stood up. "If there was a murder," he said again. "Come and be searched."

Scene Six

THE CITY ROOM of the Montreal *Clarion* was a bit like something you'd see in the movies. City rooms are not usually like that. Even at the *Clarion* you didn't have wild-eyed young cubs running across the floor yelling, 'I got a scoop!' but the rest of the picture was right – the noise and the confusion, the sloppy half-shaved characters in green eyeshades, the dirty floor, the scarred furniture and glaring lights.

Some years ago a cheapskate publisher had refused to build a special room for the teletypes, and they stood along one wall of the newsroom. Half a gross of riveters might be able to make as much noise as a row of teletypes, if they were really trying. The place was crowded, and all the characters yelled when they talked on the telephone. This was necessary because of the teletypes, and didn't add to the peace of the place.

The floor was bare as a bald head and a lot darker. The hot lights with their fanned shades beat down on a dozen littered desks, and the walls were somewhere close but cut off from light. The man at the desk nearest the window had a vest hanging open, a rumpled shirt with the top button open and the tie loosened. He had a cigar in the mouth but he didn't have a hat on the back of his head. I have yet to see a newsman wear his hat in his office, so to hell with Hollywood.

He was the night editor, and his name was Hatch. I approached him and said brightly, "I been to New York. I'm back."

He appraised me. "You look older," he decided.

"I had a poor evening. They flew the plane through the roughest weather since the one that wrecked the

Hesperus. Where is my old friend, boon drinking companion and obituary writer, MacArnold?"

"How should I know? He only works here when he isn't drinking. Have you tried your own place?"

I shook my head. "Not there. He knows I lock my liquor. I'm sorry he isn't here. I had a trade to pull."

"What did you want?"

"Oh, background on six or eight types."

"What you got to give for it? Found another body?"

"Yeah."

"Who?" he wanted to know, not too interested.

"A Senator," I told him. "Name of Cedric Kelloway. He was on the plane. He got smeared."

"I make a hobby of old Chinese tortures," Hatch said pleasantly. "You must let me show you some. *Why didn't you phone from Dorval?* The midnight is on the street and the Provincial is put to bed."

"The Redcoats are in charge," I said. "They want it should be suggested there is no story. They're not sure he was murdered. They want it buried."

"I see. If Harry Truman took a plane to England and shot the whole English cabinet with a tommy-gun, do you suppose we could manage to get it on the second front? The second front, that's the first page of the second section. Or have you forgotten everything you learned working on this newspaper?" Hatch grabbed for his telephone.

"If you're going to tell them to rip out the front page, forget it," I said. "Nobody really thinks he was killed but me. I could be wrong. All you can do is run it as accidental death, with maybe a suspicion that the R.C.M.P. are interested, unless you want to sell your presses to pay damages to the widow. She has a whole staff of lawyers who'd tell her how much to sue for."

Hatch put his telephone back.

"I wasn't in time to catch the Provincial, even phoning from Dorval, and you have the rest of the night to work it up for the City." I chuckled. "Somebody can have fun getting all the important men in the city out of bed to compose tributes."

Hatch wasn't convinced. He hated to see a good story get played down. He played me the sardonic line. He smiled, like a cat thinking about a mouse omelet. "Could we have a nice little story from you, all about how it happened?" he purred. "Something simple, with only a paragraph or so saying the Senator was probably killed. Listing the passengers, all of whom I presume, are murder suspects."

"You do what I want," I agreed, "you look up all these same passengers and tell me what you've got in the morgue or in the staff's heads about them, and I'd be glad to write you a little story. In fact, it was what I had in mind."

"In your head," Hatch corrected. "Please, don't use the word mind."

I went over to MacArnold's vacant desk, swept most of yesterday's C.P. file off the desk and pulled his mill into position. I ran a sheet of yellow copy paper into the platen of the mill, pulled out the passenger list I'd scrounged and put it on the desk, and then stared at the ceiling and tried to pull down a good lead sentence.

A card dropped on the desk.

The card was a little soiled and scuffed at the edges. It was printed in a kind of raised lettering that was supposed to look like engraving, and it said 'Rev. Horatio White, D.D.' Poised above the card was a black fat hand with broad, purple nails. Back of the hand a mountain of black vest. Above the vest a clerical collar and then a moony, glistening, bespectacled black face. It was the colored gentleman from the plane. The sickest passenger from Flight 93.

His eyes were sad and troubled. He was very worried about something. He said, "This is a very delicate situation, Brother." His voice was rich and resonant as a $1,000 radio with the tone control turned full bass.

I threw *Roget's Thesaurus* and a city directory off MacArnold's spare chair. I said, "Sit down, Doctor."

"I see you got a passenger list there, Brother."

"That's right."

"Brother, the Lord has been good to me and has made me to prosper. But I don't want my name in no newspaper."

"It won't interfere with your prosperity," I said. "I'm just writing a little story about the Senator's death. The names of those on the plane will be in the story, but nobody's going to pay any attention to them."

"Then, Brother, why put them in? Is they relevant?"

"Ah, ah. The righteous is rewarded and the wicked perish. I guess I gotta tell you a little story."

I put my feet on MacArnold's desk. I got out my State Express pack and lit one. "I've got work to do," I said. "I'll give you one cigarette."

The big Negro rolled his eyes and the whites shone in the hot light. "I been wicked, Brother," he said dolefully. "I been reveling in the fleshpots of Noo York. I drank beer and I even went to night clubs. It was a sin of weakness. I thought I paid for it on the plane. I was sick nigh unto death, and I prayed to the good Lord and he carried me through. But looks like I'm not finished paying for my backslide."

"Nobody'll notice your name," I told him. I felt a little sorry for him.

"Brother, you got to have pity on a poor sinful man. If my little flock knowed I was in Noo York, they'd run me from St. Antoine Street right into the river."

"All right, you old sinner, I'm just a softie. I'll put you

in as H. White. Plain Mr. H. White. Your flock won't get excited about that."

The Reverend Horatio smiled. The situation was softening up. The smile didn't improve his face. His teeth were so dirty they looked yellow even against his shiny blackness. And his eyes were calculating behind his glasses, even when he smiled.

He slid a thumb and finger in one vest pocket and came out with some neatly folded money. Purple money. Ten-dollar bills, three of them. He smoothed them out and shoved them at me. "That's not quite good enough, Brother," he said. "Maybe I could persuade you to leave my name off altogether. It's the last name on that list. It would be an easy mistake to make."

I looked at the money for a minute. It wasn't the kind of money I had in my handkerchief pocket. It wasn't even the kind of money I was used to seeing; it was dirtier. I leaned forward and butted my cigarette. "What do you think I am, a reporter?" I asked him? "I'm not. I make money. That lets me do the jobs I want, the way I want to. Right now I want to see your name in that paper. It could be interesting. Reverend Horatio White. I might even put in your degree. Doctor of Divinity. Where'd you get it, from a correspondence school?"

The big preacher sighed with a rumble like Vesuvius burping. "I guess I gotta tell you another little story, Brother."

"Nope. The cigarette's out."

"But Brother, you wouldn't want to ruin an innocent man. Lissen. They was a big mortgage on our poor little church for many long years. The men that held that mortgage was worried. Then I was called by the Lord to minister at this little church. Through my efforts, my in-de-fa-tig-a-bul efforts, that mortgage was paid off. Not only the interest, Brother. The whole thing. We burned it. And natcherly, the men that held that mortgage was grateful to me. They showed their gratitude handsomely, brother, and so I went on a little trip to Noo York. Now, they was nothing wrong in that. The good Lord don't say it's wrong to take an envelope when someone holds it out to you. But my flock don't think that way. A few of the brethren has nasty minds. If they knew I was in Noo York…"

"Do they read the *Clarion*?"

"Brother, I fear they does."

"Then they'll know. It's as simple as that."

Horatio thumbed his vest again and came out with another fold of purple bills. There were two. That made fifty dollars. "It's not quite that simple," he said.

The bills had the wrong effect on me. I got mad. I stood up and said, "Blow. Or I'll show you the broken door to the elevator shaft."

"Don't be hasty," he pleaded.

"You be hasty. Be damn' hasty."

The Reverend White smiled. "Razor blades," he said. "Dark streets. Don't be hasty, Brother. Your work keeps you out late nights. And I got lots of friends."

"Tell 'em I carry a gun."

"You ever seen a man mugged? A mugger works from behind. He don't worry if you got a gun."

"Yes, I've seen a man mugged," I said. "Have you ever seen the inside of a church?"

He shook his head slowly, with deep sadness for me. "Sometimes it pays to believe, Brother," he said. "The unbeliever perisheth. Late at night on a dark street, he perisheth."

He picked up his money and put it carefully back in his vest, like a mother kangaroo retrieving an errant child.

Then he got up and clumped out of the city room. Nobody watched him go. An Arab chief in full burnoose might attract attention in that city room, but not a Negro minister.

I got the city directory off the floor. There was a Rev. Horatio White listed, at 415 Hyslop Street. That was a few blocks west of Guy, probably just below St. Antoine. I went over to see Hatch. "Is Hole Willie still your church editor?" I asked.

"Yep. But it's Monday night, so naturally he isn't around."

"I'll find him," I said. I wandered off and got his number from a reporter and phoned him. It rang about eight times.

"Hello," a sleepy voice said.

"Comrade, this is the *Clarion*."

The church editor was a retired minister who did newspaper work for pin money. He didn't like it. "Really!" he said. "What time is it?"

"Never mind, Comrade. This is why we pay you. I need something for a story. Ever hear of the Reverend Horatio White?"

"Yes." He was terse. He was tight-lipped. He was going to be hell for the regular staffers to work with for a month.

"Go on," I said.

"He sends me a copy of his sermon every week."

"Does he ever preach the sermons?"

"Frankly, I hope not. But there's no reason why he shouldn't. He has a pulpit. The African Church of the Lost Lamb, on St. Antoine."

"What kind of a church?"

"About what you'd expect. Shabby. But there's money in the congregation somewhere. They had a mortgage bigger than the church. Some sharks were holding it. It was paid off just a few months ago – in a lump sum."

"Thanks, comrade," I said. "That's just bully. Sleep on."

After that the next thing I did was type out a copy of the passenger list and give it to Hatch. "Try to remember the old days before you had your lobectomy, and make like a newsman with this batch," I asked him.

I went back to MacArnold's mill and rolled out a nice little story, no purple overtones, about how Kelloway died. It was a long time since I'd done anything like that and it was a no by-line story. Hatch would wear out a lot of blue pencil on it. But it told the facts, which I knew better than anyone.

Hatch came over and sat beside me just as I was finishing. I hauled the last yellow sheet out of the mill and then folded up the whole story and put it in my pocket. He liked that the way little boys like padlocked cookie jars. "Hey, give," he said unpleasantly. "We're in a hurry."

"So'm I. Pay me first."

He tried to outstare me, but I knew just how tough he was, and besides I didn't work for him any more. He went back to his desk for the copy of the passenger list and then sat down again and gave it to me.

"Florence Milsky. Who was she?"

"I'm asking you," I told him. "By elimination, she was uglier than anything you'd want to see, tall as I am and with more bone than a small-mouthed bass. Which she resembled. Dark, thin, and her bile-blower was working overtime even before she got sick. What you got on her?"

"Nothing. She must be from New York or somewhere. Next, Mrs. H.J. Smythe. Old dame?"

"Yep. Old club-woman. More money on her fingers in old-fashioned settings than there is in any safety deposit box on St. James Street."

"That's her," Hatch said. "Wife of the Smythe who could nickel-plate his whole house, if he wanted to. Or galvanize it – he owns most of the zinc around here, too. Age fifty-three, maiden name Derby, native Montrealer – or Westmounter. Okay?"

"Check."

"Donald Willcot ... " he began.

"You can skip him just now. How about this guy Scarper?"

"Scarper. There you got something fishy," he said. He sounded unhappy. "I've tried to find out about him before now. He was mixed up in a fast switch that was pulled on some paper company stocks here last winter. Seems as though he engineered a deal by which a syndicate bought up enough stock to throw out the management and put in new ones. There were some poor, beat-up old $50,000-a-year men standing in the breadlines afterward, very unhappy. But we got nothing at all on him for a story, and he dropped out of sight. Here he is again. I bet he killed the Senator."

"Sure," I said, "but let's just sift the others."

"Sift them, they fall right through," he said. "What you got? Lorette Toledo, you know who she is. A French-Canadian manufacturer's agent with a wife and seven kids in Outrement, name of Aime LaRouche, who goes back and forth to New York every fortnight. Horatio White – you say you did him yourself. And Charles Garnett. There's a suspect for you. Fairly old guy, eh, with a face like old Rover the retriever?"

"Check."

"Please stop saying check," he begged me politely. "You sound like a goddam chess player. And Charles Garnett. You know who Charles Garnett is? The Montreal bureau chief of International Press. Will that be all?"

"I'm glad there was one newsman on the plane," I said. "It gives me a lead to work on."

"Ha, ha. No kidding, who did it?"

"Don't tell anybody, but it was the pilot."

"You kill me. Why were you on the plane?"

"I wanted my stomach flushed out," I said, "and I couldn't find a stomach pump."

"Why were you in New York?"

"Here," I said. I gave him the story. It stopped his questions.

I sat there for a minute, alone in the clatter and the yelling, trying to think. There were two things to think about. The first and most important was, who was Ann's father? The late Senator, or Charles Garnett, or even Scarper?

Then, who killed Kelloway? If he was really killed, and if he was Ann's father, I could probably have to tie up with that one. Otherwise Dorset could have it all.

So the first thing to find out was, who was Ann's father?

I had lots of leads on that. Oh, lots. She wouldn't even tell me who her mother was. And her name, Wedgewood, was clearly a phoney even though it was the one she operated under in New York.

It suddenly struck me with full force that I didn't even know her exact age. Maybe I should go back to New York and start again. Maybe, but I'd be damned if I would.

Scene Seven

IT WAS ABOUT THREE O'CLOCK when I finished the story and left the *Clarion* office. I walked a few blocks just to get the newsroom air out of my lungs. It was going to be a nice morning. Mid-September in Montreal, and the storm had washed and crisped up the air, the way a water spray revives lettuce. We were probably due now for a spell of Indian autumn, before we were warmed up again with Indian summer. After that, it would get cold enough to freeze the chops off a St. Bernard but then the snow would come and I could ski. Good old Montreal.

I loved the peace and quiet of the Montreal night, the quiet broken only by the low-flying zoom of cruising taxicabs, the peace broken only by the crash and smash of bottles and bellhops being thrown out of hotel room windows.

I walked up Windsor Street. At 3:10, cold sober, I stood at the corner of Windsor and Dorchester. That was a most unusual set of circumstances, and there were undesirable angles to it. I was tired; and I was cold sober.

If I walked to St. Catherine Street and Atwater, I would get to Dorset's office at 3:30, just when he wanted me. It was a lovely night for walking. What I did was duck into a small supposedly closed bar on Dorchester, work my way quietly through a very cold quart of Molson and then take a taxi to R.C.M.P. headquarters. Maybe it wasn't the healthy alternative, but my health has to watch out for itself.

I blame what happened afterward on the quart of Molson. Perhaps I am being unfair to John H.R. Molson and Bros. Perhaps the impulse would have got the better of me anyhow. But you always try to blame something except yourself.

R.C.M.P. headquarters was a long, low yellow-brick building – actually it had been converted from a wartime light manufacturing plant – on St. Catherine's west of Atwater. The street was broad here, and there were no cars in sight except one canary-colored Cadillac convertible drawn up at the entrance to headquarters. The cabby pulled up just past the convertible and I paid him off and walked back.

Sitting in the convertible was a girl with a face I had seen often before. She had long, flowing real blonde hair. Her face was tanned far darker than the hair and her sun-bleached eyebrows cut two white slashes in its glowing darkness. Her face was too long for its width and too strong for its purpose. It was a face with strong will but no character, intense desire but no appreciation, great beauty and small intelligence.

The lipstick on her firm mouth was black in the night and black against her dark face. Her lips were parted and her white teeth gleamed toward me for no purpose, not smiling, not showing any emotion. She had no emotion. She was all will.

She was spoiled top-drawer Westmount, upper level. She needed someone to slap her often across her beauti-fully smooth, hard face. Mauling might bring her around, but just now she was so used to getting her own way and following her own fancies that life bored her completely.

She looked about old enough to have come out at the last St. Andrews Ball before the war. She would play a good game of golf and an unspeakable game of bridge. She would have a good seat in the saddle and would know something about yachting. Her clothes were too perfect to be true. Not a spot, not a crease, not one compromise to the ordinary world, like an expertly-retouched picture. She had a casual, sexy figure and they were casual-sexy clothes; they let her skin shine through in unexpected places and gave the impression there was nothing underneath them. You felt she would shuck them off with no effort, and almost no prompting. She was the kind of woman who causes unpremeditated rape.

She always did whatever she wanted to, because the word 'consequences' was not in her vocabulary. There never were any consequences for her. She was Carol Kelloway, the Senator's only seed.

I looked at her. I'd seen her picture often enough and I'd seen her before, but I'd never met her.

I knew without being told that I could avoid more trouble than I'd ever been in, just by not speaking to her.

"Hello, Carol," I said.

She looked at me then as a person, instead of just something spoiling her view. I looked about six feet tall. I looked as if I had black hair, brushed back but not slicked down, and a tanned face with heavy black eyebrows, straight nose, kind of gaunt cheeks and a chin I could lead with if I had to. I didn't look like a football player, but I also didn't look as if a welterwight boxer could tear me apart. I looked like someone she couldn't order around without an argument. That was guaranteed to intrigue her.

"Hello. Sit down," she said.

The convertible top was down. The canary Cadillac had black leather seats, shiny as though no one had ever sat on them. There was a faint throb of music inside the car, a radio turned very low. I opened the door and got in.

"You know about your father," I said.

"Yes." The voice was expressionless. Father is dead, it meant, and might as well be forgotten.

"Why did he go to New York?"

"Who are you?"

"I'm a skip-chaser," I said, "an eye, a Humphrey Bogart role. I'm the face on the bartender's lap."

"Who are you?" she asked again in the same dead tone.

"Nobody. I was on the same plane with your father."

"How would I know why he went to New York?"

"I don't suppose you would," I said. It wasn't supposed to be a compliment and it wasn't made to sound like one. The tone I used made her look at me with a little interest. She wore no makeup except her lipstick and the light gleamed on her smooth, flat cheeks as she turned. Only the expression on her face was spoiled; the structure was Grade A prime.

"Let's go somewhere and talk." She started the engine and had the car doing fifty along the street before I could tell her I was supposed to go see Dorset.

Dorset could wait a while.

One of the Negro clubs near St. Antoine Street has a little downstairs bar where you can find more voluntarily-unemployed money spenders than in the Ritz Cafe. The room is long and dark and shabby. It's dirty, but not dirty enough to smell. The little tables are solid and heavy and have been nailed to the floor ever since the Neurological Institute complained; the chairs are movable, but they're light and rickety and won't break heads. There is a short bar and a small piano. Someone is always behind the bar, and someone is from time to time in front of the piano, playing too softly to disturb anyone. I used to like the place five years ago, before it got too popular with my friends.

That was where we went.

Carol ordered a brandy and soda. I had beer. There are places where I like my drinks to come out of sealed bottles.

She did considerable damage to her drink in two long inhalations. Then suddenly she began to talk. It came out in a tight, strained voice that was through pretending it didn't care. "You don't like me," she began. "You think I don't feel anything about his death. Well, you're wrong. Sometimes people get so used to not letting things show that they freeze, even if they want to break wide open. I'm frozen."

"You're beginning to show some cracks," I said.

"The Senator was a pal of mine. Believe me, I want to know who killed him. And the police? They don't even think he was killed." She went on and referred to the police in phrases she'd picked up from the stable-boys on days when the horses were nervous.

I waited for her to cool down. I let her rant on and didn't even listen; I knew exactly what I thought of the police, myself, and her attitude wasn't going to influence mine.

I looked around the bar. It should have been full of people I knew. By odd coincidence, it wasn't. There was no one there I'd ever seen before. No one, that is, except two people I'd happened to meet this same evening.

Lorette Toledo and her pal Mr. Scarper were at the end table, beside the piano. They were both drinking something tall, pink, sickly and loaded with fruit salad out of tall tapering glasses. They looked typical. The dim light made Lorette look more bleached than blonde and it made Scarper look more blue-rinsed than graying. They were what you might call an assorted pair; ill-assorted. They made me so sick I came back to my spoiled acquaintance.

I asked Carol, "So the police don't think your father was killed. So why don't they?"

"No weapon," she said.

"No weapon?"

"Look, you were there, weren't you? My father was

killed by a blow on the head. A blow delivered by something hard and heavy — the old traditional blunt instrument. Or if he wasn't killed that way, he fell and hit his head."

"Sure," I said.

"Well, the inspector told me they searched every person on that plane. And they searched the plane. They even searched the luggage in the luggage compartment, though it seemed impossible that anyone could hide a weapon there before the plane landed. And they found nothing."

"No blunt instrument."

"Nothing that would even raise a small bump."

"I wonder ..." I said. I let the sentence trail off to appear mysterious, but I really didn't have anything more to say.

She was excited about the affair. She was too hard to show grief, even if she felt it, but there was something else — some tense, worried drive behind her thoughts.

"But I know he was murdered," she said. "The police must have been stupid enough to miss the weapon. So they advance this absurd theory that he fell and injured himself. They say that because they don't think there were any reasons for his murder. They don't think anyone on the plane had any motive to murder him. That is where they're wrong."

"And there were reasons for killing him?" I asked her. "That's my girl. That's what I want to know. Tell me."

"Who are you?"

"Later on you can look me up in Who's Who, but right now I want all you know."

"There was something very funny about this trip," she said, and told the story speaking quickly and jerkily. The Senator had gone to the office as usual the previous Thursday morning. Just after lunch he'd phoned home and asked

Mrs. Kelloway to have a bag packed for him. He was going to New York by plane that afternoon.

"Willcot came around for the bag at four o'clock," Carol said, "and I saw him for a minute. I had a date to play golf with the Senator that afternoon and I was annoyed at being stood up, so I asked him the reason for the sudden trip."

She had finished her second brandy and I used my eyes to bring the waiter with another. She seemed to have some method of passing the stuff through her stomach without getting it into her bloodstream; there wasn't the slightest glaze to her gaze.

She went on, "Don Willcot told me the Senator had received a call from New York late in the morning. There was a long conversation and when he hung up he was worried and in a foul mood. He didn't tell Don the subject of the call, but he kept thinking about something and couldn't attend to his work. Finally at lunchtime he called in the vice-presidents of Kelloway Metals, told them just what to do to clean up the dozen-odd things that were on the fire for the rest of that week, and said he was called unexpectedly to the New York office on a vital matter ..."

"He said he was called to the New York office, not that he was called to New York?" I asked, to get the point clear.

"Yes. So Don reported. Then he told Don to get plane reservations for both of them that afternoon, and had him phone the New York manager to say they were coming and would need hotel accommodations, and to give the arrival time."

"What hotel did they stay at?"

"The Waldorf, I suppose."

"I suppose so," I agreed. "Did you ever hear the name Wedgewood?"

"No. Who is that?"

"It's a nice young girl in New York."

"Father's weakness was controlling corporations," she said. "He didn't have any nice young girls in New York."

"I wasn't suggesting he did," I said patiently. "Have you seen Willcot this evening?"

"He came to the house to tell us of father's death. I woke mother and told her."

"Uh-huh. Well, what happened in New York?"

She did a good job of portraying cold outrage. "Willcot came to tell me my father had been killed. Do you think I felt like asking him a bunch of silly questions?"

"I bet you fool a lot of people," I said. "Sure, you asked. For two reasons. One, because you were suspicious of the trip to begin with. Two, because you are now convinced the Senator was murdered, which means you know more than you've told me so far. Give."

Her varnished blonde coldness stayed in place. She admitted I was right without giving any sign she was admitting. "I found out it wasn't an ordinary business trip," she told me. "For one thing, when Willcot and the Senator arrived at LaGuardia the New York manager met them and asked father why he'd come. He gave a very flimsy reason, Don says. And most of the time they were there, the Senator was out around the town on business he didn't disclose to Don. Don was staying by the telephone in the hotel room, which struck him as peculiar because usually the New York trips mean long conferences in the New York office and Don has to sit in and take notes."

"I see," I said. For something to say.

"Perhaps you see, but what are you going to do about it? Why do you want to do anything about it, anyhow? Why are you involving yourself in this?"

"I told you. I'm a private detective, looking for business. The police don't believe your father was murdered.

I'm willing to believe it. I'm even willing to look for his murderer."

"For a fee," she said, in a tone of voice which could hit a cuspidor at ten feet.

"Not from you," I told her. "I've already got a fee. I got this fee to investigate something your father may have been involved in. I have to investigate him anyway, and I'll take on the investigation of his death as a side-line."

"Why are you investigating him?"

"It's nothing that'll do him any harm, now he's dead, even if he really was involved."

"Could it have caused his death?"

I thought for a minute. I tried to tie things together. I drank a whole glass of my beer to oil the wheels, but the pieces didn't tie. Maybe Senator Kelloway was Ann Wedgewood's father. Maybe he'd been threatening Margaret, Ann's mother. Had Margaret been on the plane? Was she, for instance, Mrs. H. K. Smythe, the old dowager? It was an interesting thought. But it didn't make any difference, because neither Margaret nor Mrs. Smythe was the kind to do murder. And anyhow there was no weapon, which meant there was no murder. Or did it?

To a point, it added up. The Senator made a mysterious trip to New York. Margaret made a mysterious trip to New York because she was meeting the father of her first-born. That could make them lover and loved – there aren't that many people who make mysterious trips from Montreal to New York. But it still didn't get the Senator killed.

Maybe the Senator made his mysterious trip for another purpose altogether, a purpose that resulted in his being killed. Assuming he was killed, that is, and waltz me around again Willie. That could make either Scarper or old dog-puss Garnett the father of Ann the banded redhead.

Nope, nothing tied. Carol was getting bored watching

me think. Everything was negative, so I replied in that vein.

"No, it couldn't have caused his death," I said.

"What are you investigating?"

"I won't tell you," I said, not nicely. "I won't take a fee from you and I won't work for you. If I find out something about your father's death it'll be from my own foolish curiosity, not as a favor for you. I don't like you. If you want me to, I'll put it stronger than that. I've known a lot of girls of your general social class and disposition and I've never liked any of them, and you, Blondie, come from a higher level of Westmount than any of them."

"Who are you?"

"We've been through that," I said.

"What's your name?"

"Teed," I told her. "Russell Teed."

She smiled. It wasn't a pleasant smile. It was a cougar thinking of breakfast, getting ready to spring on a fawn. "I've heard of you," she said. "I didn't realize you were the great Russell Teed. I want you to forget everything I've told you. I don't want you to do anything about my father's murder. I'll even pay you to forget your other case, the one that makes you want to investigate him. How much money would you want?"

"I take money for doing things, not for forgetting about them," I said.

"How much? How much to keep out of this whole thing? I don't want you anywhere near the case. I hate the inside of jails."

"What do you mean?" But I knew what she meant.

"Inez Scaley," she said. "Inez Scaley Sark. You must remember her. She's an old friend of mine – we grew up on the same street. Tell me about the time you were investigating her husband's murder. She gave me the whole story at the time, but I'm afraid I've forgotten some of it. About how you had her put in jail for the murder, when she was supposed to be your client. Tell me about that part."

"I got her out again. And we found the real murderer. I couldn't help the police putting her in the pokey. She lied to me. She didn't kill her husband but she had opportunity to do it. She forgot to tell me that, and when the police found out, I couldn't protect her."

"I might lie to you too," Carol said. "I sometimes do lie, when I have to, you know. Then you'd have me put in jail."

"You could hardly have killed your father," I pointed out. "You weren't on the plane."

"I was disguised as the co-pilot," she said.

"Sure. And you brought along a golf club and swatted the Senator because you were sore at him for breaking that golf date."

"Sure. And then dropped it out the luggage port."

"Shall we get back to earth? Or has the brandy backed up to your brain at last?"

She grasped her purse and pushed back her chair. "I'm leaving," she said. "You keep out of this. If you want to be paid to keep out, I'll pay you. If not I'll find some other way to stop you."

"I promise not to hang the murder on you."

She stood up. "There'll be other murders," she predicted calmly, "before this is all over."

"Appearances are all wrong," I said, amazed. "You know something. You know something more about this than you've told."

She went all serious and grim on me. It suited her. It seemed natural to the type of face she'd been cultivating all these years. "The Senator hadn't anyone to confide in," she said. "He couldn't talk to mother. She didn't understand anything. I was the only one who ever got inside him. I knew that man and the way he ran things, so well I could take over his whole empire today if I wanted to. Because I run myself the same way he operated. I have a carbon copy of his code."

Fathering Ann Wedgewood was something the Senator wouldn't tell his wife. Whether or not she had general understanding, she wouldn't understand that. What kind of things did he confide to his little diamond daughter?

"Business," I said. "He used to tell you all about his business?"

"His business. And everything."

"And he told you what kind of business he was going to New York to do? Or was it business?"

"When I think back over some things he told me lately," she said slowly, "I'm sure I know why he went. It was business. Of a sort."

"We must get together sometime over a bottle of Old Smokey and straighten out our thinking," I said sweetly. "Define terms, for instance. 'Business of a sort', for instance."

"It would be so nice. But we won't be meeting again, didn't I tell you?"

She slammed her empty chair back to the table. She rocked the table, and my beer bottle tried to fall over. I caught it in both hands. When I looked up again she was gone. I was sorry I'd missed the exit. Then when I thought it over, I wasn't sorry. She was so beautiful even from behind I probably would have gone running after her.

It is easy to get killed in various ways. Some people love liquor so much it kills them. With others it's food, and there are even some people crazy enough to exercise themselves to death. Oscar Wilde thought he was being smart when he said you always kill the thing you love. Nuts. The thing you love always kills you, or almost always. It would be that way with her.

She was so poisonous you didn't have to love her to get killed, to get sucked soulless. Just being around her was enough. She was poison, a particularly bitter, challenging sort of poison – 'I dare you to take me'. She was the only living thing in her world, and anything that touched her was just her chattel. Humanity should be an end in itself, but in her world everything was a means to her end. I wondered what her end would be. I couldn't imagine her dying.

Sure, she could run her father's business. She could run Stalin's Russia, if she wanted to.

It wasn't idle thought, all this. It wasn't something I'd picked up in our little chat, either. I knew all about her. I'd seen her lash to death a horse who wouldn't jump. I'd seen her drive three men to uselessness. One of them I knew too well.

I congratulated myself on meeting her, just simply meeting her, and not having anything bad happen.

I congratulated myself too soon.

Scene Eight

It was cool and pleasant in the little Negro bar, and there was a colored man tinkling the piano softly and nostalgically, sort of like Oscar Paterson in a wistful mood. The bar was called The Caravan – nobody knew why. Nobody ever knows why bars are called what they are. The waiters criss-crossed the room, walking rhythmically and silently like rubber-shoed players on a tennis court.

My beer was cold. It sat in the tall glass with just a thin froth of foam overlying it, and the little carbonation bubbles rushing in flights to the surface like sandpipers jetting from one sand bar to the next, and drops of water condensing on the outside and tracing hesitant, jerky, crooked little paths to the table. Nothing is more beautiful than a glass of cold beer when you are thirsty and tired and contented.

I was all of that. I was even contented. The case didn't worry me that much. Senator Kelloway was dead, probably murdered, but aside from that it was a calm, undisturbing, non-violent case. Even the Senator had been killed very quietly and neatly. That was appropriate. He had been a neat little man.

Scarper, on the other hand, was not neat.

I looked at him, sitting some distance away from me, with the garishly blonde Lorette Toledo sitting across from him. They were having a confidential tete-a-tete, leaning toward each other over the table-top. If they leaned much farther their necks would get tangled together.

They seemed to feel me watching them. Their heads slowly rotated toward me, in perfect unison like a head and its mirror image. Like a reflection in one of those hangover blue mirrors they use in modern decorating –

one yellow head, one blue head.

They must have been talking about me. The expressions on them as they stared at me were downright hangdog. Not anxious nor embarrassed nor even guilty, but concerned. They had been talking about me and trying to decide what to do about me and there I was, still there, still watching them. Hawkshaw Teed. They would have to do something about old Hawkshaw. They were just deciding specifically what.

I was a little annoyed. I didn't want them doing anything about me. And I objected to them having secret conferences all over the place, but always just out of my hearing. They were an unexplained angle to the plane trip, and they might easily have something to do with Kelloway's death. They had been busy enough in the little room at LaGuardia, whispering and discussing their fellow passengers. And Lorette, on Scarper's prompting, had spoken to Willcot and told him something about one of the other passengers.

It was another piece of the puzzle. And like every piece I'd come across so far, it had rough edges and didn't match the rough edges of any other piece.

I wanted a long, unpleasant talk with those two. I decided I was going to accost them. Right away. Of course, I set to work to finish my beer first.

A colored boy came into the room, looked around slowly, and then came over and sat down at my table. When we came in, Carol and I had taken a table for four. Now I was alone at the table, so there was plenty of room. At the same time there were plenty of empty tables around the room and I didn't see why he couldn't sit at one of them. I didn't say so, though.

He ordered a beer and sat back comfortably in his chair. He reached slowly into his pocket, brought out an unopened pack of cigarettes and began neatly and deliberately to open it up. He was a nice-looking boy, well dressed but not jazzed up in the Harlem way. His dark-brown tropical suit was a conservative cut, he had a white shirt and I have seen louder ties in the St. James Club. His only odd characteristic was his combination of colour and fine features. He was as black as any human has ever been, a shiny, buffed, bone-deep blackness, but his face was almost Caucasian. Then lips, a nose more sharp than flat and broad, a forehead that did not bulge. He was too black for an Arab and too smooth-haired for an African; he was perhaps a product of the native race-mixture in Jamaica or Trinidad.

He got his cigarettes unwrapped and pulled one from the pack. Then he began groping for a match. He didn't seem to have a match.

"I beg your pardon," he said hesitantly. His voice was soft and a little slurred, but not Southern United States. "I wonder if I might have a light?"

I looked at him. I shook my head. I don't feel I have to justify myself. There was work for me to do, and I wasn't in a mood to talk without purpose.

"I don't make friends that easy," I said.

He smiled. His teeth were small and crooked and white. "No offense," he said genially. He pulled out a match folder and lit his smoke.

I sat. The piano player could have been smoking reefers, because his playing got frenzied, in a genteel way. I kept at my beer but I didn't hurry. Scarper and Toledo were still sitting there and showed no sign of leaving. I could get to them before they got their necks pried apart, in case they decided to go. I hauled out my State Express pack and had a cigarette myself, after the friendly colored boy had stopped using the ashtray.

Two more colored youths came into the room. They were two for the books. One wore a checkerboard-pattern sport jacket and the other a deep pink rayon tropical suit. They checkerboard had a bow-tie big enough to choke a mail chute and the pink suit was pointed up with a florescent lavender tie. They waved to my companion and he beckoned. They came over and sat down, one on each side of him. That also put them one on each side of me.

"Hi-hi, Petey," the checkerboard said. "We come right as soon as you phoned. Nice place."

The pink suit stayed silent. He was tall and heavy and black with a coarse bone structure to his face and firm thick flesh overlaid in blobs. His lips were thicker than my thumb and stayed half-open over great yellowed fangs. He didn't look as though he could talk if he wanted to.

"I'm glad you and Bing could come," my first friend told Checkers. "I hope you haven't been working too hard today. We have something to do."

There was no answer to that, so in the lull I spoke up. "Gee, fellows, I'm sorry," I said. "I didn't know I'd taken your favorite table. Why don't I just move over to one of these empty tables here? Unless you'd like to, of course."

All three of them turned and stared at me. And that was all they did. Sometimes it doesn't pay to be nice.

"Look," I said, "there are plenty of empty tables. All I want is to be left alone. I'm not friendly. I'm not a writer, so I don't care to stay here and listen to your conversation to use it for dialogue. Will you move on? I was here first."

They stared. Bing stirred slightly, as though he was reaching into a deep pocket, but nothing else happened.

"Do I have to make a scene?"

They stared. They waited for me to make a scene.

"Okay," I said. "I know when I'm licked." I got my beer bottle in one hand and my glass in the other and started to shove back my chair. "You don't mind if I leave you?" I asked politely.

A hand came down on my knee with a little less weight than a pneumatic hammer. At the same time something long and thin rested across my upper leg, as though someone had laid a pencil there. Only it was sharper than a pencil.

Petey, the man who had first sat down with me, smiled and said, "Please stay."

I set down my beer glass.

"We'd hate to have you leave," Petey said. "And that's a razor Bing's holding against your leg. Not a safety razor, one of the old kind. With a very long blade. He only has to shift his hand an inch to get that artery, that big artery that runs down the inside of your leg there."

Bing took his hand off my knee. But that slight pressure against my upper leg remained. Now I knew whatever it was it felt sharp enough to go right through the bone.

I set down my beer bottle.

Checkers picked up my beer bottle and filled my glass with it. He held my glass a funny way while he was filling it. He held his hand half up over the top of the glass. He could have been dropping something in it.

"Let's all have a drink," Petey said. He beckoned the waiter. "Two more glasses," he said politely, "and beer all around, Jack."

So he knew the waiter. The waiter was Jack. Jack smiled politely back at Petey and bowed slightly while he took the order. Everyone was being very goddamned polite. And it was clearly not going to get me anywhere to complain to that waiter. Or to ask him for the headwaiter. Of course, I could always yell.

"You wouldn't start anything, would you?" Petey asked me. He was clairvoyant. "You wouldn't like to bleed to death. All that would happen, if you yelled, Bing would slash you and we'd run out. Bing knows right where to slash. You'd pass out from loss of blood before a doctor or anyone who knew anything could get here, and you'd bleed to death. It would save us an awful lot of trouble. But you wouldn't yell."

I lied in my teeth. "Nothing was farther from my mind." After I'd lied in my teeth, I clamped them together. They were showing a slight inclination to chatter.

"Why don't you drink up your beer, Russy?" Petey suggested. "Go ahead."

I shook my head. "What's the idea?" I said.

"You'll find out later."

"I'll wait till I find out."

There was a sound, a slight sound that you could best describe as a *snick*. I don't really care how you describe it. I wasn't concerned with the sound, but only with the feeling that went with it. The feeling was a sting, and then an ooze. Bing's razor in one short, effortless stroke had cut through the weave of my pants and into my skin. From the sting I judged there was a shallow gash three or four inches across my leg. From the ooze I judged there was going to be lots of blood spilling around. And the razor lay in the open gash burning and ready to cut deeper.

Petey was looking at me kindly. "You see what would happen if you tried to get up," he said. "You'd practically cut your own leg off. And don't think about knocking Bing's hand away. You have no idea how strong and quick he is. Go ahead, have some beer."

"You won't do anything," I told him steadily. I had fought up from the horror of the naked steel. Now I was getting mad. "You've got orders to bring me in, haven't you? You wouldn't kill me here. Tell me the story. Maybe I'll come willing."

"Oh," he said, and shook his head, "oh you're so wrong. We got orders to bring you in. But we can kill you if you don't come, and we won't even get our knuckles rapped. Our boss isn't that particular."

I leaned forward toward him. The razor twisted in the open cut and I almost gagged from its feel. "You look like you ought to be your own boss," I said. "You and I ought to be able to talk this over."

He was still shaking his head. "No, Russy, you just drink your beer. When I work for a man, I'm smart enough to work for him. When I have a job to do I do it. You just drink up. You'll only get a little drunk from that beer. Why," he said kindly, "you'll be better off after you drink that than you are now."

I stared at Petey. I tried to figure some way out. He was a clean, healthy, educated man with a good sense of process. He knew how to get things done. He wasn't worried about all this at all. It was his way of operating, and maybe it wasn't orthodox but it worked. He had me. All I had to do was drink the beer, and they could carry me away. I could stall, but it wouldn't get me anything. It would just lose me blood.

"We ain't got all night, has we?" Checkers asked suddenly. He looked at Bing as he spoke.

Then I felt the steel push deeper into my left. I felt the flesh part under it. I felt it meeting the resistance of tendon and I felt the tendon begin to part. Bing's hand was strong as a tantalum alloy and the razor was sharper than your maiden aunt's tongue.

I picked up my glass. So I could stall. Who'd rescue me? Scarper and Toledo? Yeah, sure.

"Relax," I said. I took a swig. The pressure on my leg eased.

Then they just sat and watched me and waited. Pretty

soon everything that struck my senses began to change color. First everything was pale lilac; then deep mauve; then dark purple. The table and the glasses and bottles on it were dark purple, and Petey was dark purple, and the piano was playing dark purple music. There was a dark purple ringing in my head and a dark purple taste in my mouth.

Bing took the razor away and stopped cutting me.

The last thing I saw was Scarper's dark purple face turned toward me. It was grinning.

That was just before the dark purple turned to dead black.

The blackness seemed to endure for only a few instants. Then something not black, but a very dark grey, impinged on my ears. I concentrated on it; it was all I had to concentrate on. It was some kind of dull and doleful music.

It was organ music. Not Hammond electric, but genuine church or movie palace. It was playing something as sad as a Hebrew lullaby or a Highland lament. I opened my eyes, and I was sitting in church in the front pew.

I was crazy. Whatever they'd fed me was loaded with the stuff opium dreams are made of.

I wasn't crazy. I was sitting in the front pew in church.

Every fifteen or sixteen seconds, with the regularity of a rotating marine light, someone soaked me across the face with a wet towel. It was a pale mauve wet towel. I was better.

Voices confirmed this. "He's coming out," someone said. I squinted toward the voice, and it was Petey. The towel hit me once more and then stopped. The organ music got louder.

"What's that for?" I asked in a drunk voice. "To drown my screams?"

"There won't be no screams, Brother," a rich set of tubes told me.

I squinted again. There, as I might have suspected, was the Reverend Horatio White.

"You reassure me," I said.

Looking around, I couldn't tell how I'd known it was a church when I first woke up. The place was so dimly lighted it was hardly lit at all. Ahead of me three steps led up to the chancel and in there, behind and above the dull wood altar, was a great stained glass window. Most of the glass looked deep purple in the dimness. I closed my eyes quickly, and the dismal organ music beat into my ringing ears.

So I was in the African Church of the Lost Lamb. I didn't have to strain myself to guess that.

The sonorous drone of the Reverend White's voice came very dimly to me. I guess I was in poor shape, because if anyone would know the acoustics of that church to the last decibel, he would. "You is a very fortunate man, Brother," he was telling me. "You was warned, and you persisted stubborn in the error of your way. Now you is come to judgment, but your judgment is merciful."

"Thanks," I managed.

"I want you to know you is forgiven," he persisted. "I been thinkin' of a suitable punishment for you, since you was foolish enough to try to ruin my place in this church, and put to naught all my good works here. But I come to the conclusion that God will punish you enough."

"Not God as much as Nature," I told him. "I expect nature makes most people feel like this when they've been Mickeyed."

"Just one little warning, Brother," he orated on. "Don't stay tangled up with any of this business that happened on that there plane. Forget me and forget everyone else who was on that there plane. I feel very, very sure you will do that, won't you, Brother? Because you seen how easy it is for poor sinners that don't mind their own business to get hurted. You is getting off with just a warnin' brother, because I is a kind man."

"With a warning," I said. "And a nicked knee. And a laudanum headache. I'll remember you zombies."

Petey came back into the picture. Polite as usual. "Careful," he said. "You've been very lucky, so far."

I turned my head toward him. When the back of my neck stopped creaking and I could hear myself, I said "You're the prize kiss-off boy in this picture. You're too smart to be working for this old witch doctor. Come around and see me and I'll give you a job myself, if you could bring yourself to turn honest."

The Reverend Horatio shook his head at me sadly. "You is bein' ungrateful, brother. I been kind and forbearing with you, but watch out."

He stuck his face up close to mine. It was soft and greasy. It was not very clean and it announced that by its smell. "Just mind your step, Brother," he chanted. "Walk in the way of the righteous. And fo'get all about us."

"If there's one thing I'm beginning to get tired of," I said sleepily, "it's being told to forget things. Sometimes I wish I could forget."

I blinked at the great round fat face so close to my eyes. It was blurred, but that wasn't what bothered me. What bothered me was its color. It was slowly changing from purple-black to purple-purple. I blinked again. It was pure deep purple. So was anything else I could see. I was on the way out again.

It wasn't really necessary, but they helped me along. Just as things were turning black there was that blinding flash of light at the back of my eyeballs that meant one of them had hit me on the head.

Scene Nine

ONCE OR TWICE, I suppose, in a lifetime you go through experiences you don't expect to live through. Sometimes you don't even want to live through them. Then when you have had bad dreams they come back to you and you go through all the tortures of hell again, just as you did the first time.

I found myself back on my rubber raft in the North Atlantic. I had been on the raft almost three days, through an autumn gale, and I was so close to dead I'd lost any will to live. The only ones who got out of the plane at all when it went into the drink were the tail-gunner and I, and he'd washed off the raft sometime the second night.

No one had ever been so wet and so cold before and stayed conscious, and I wasn't fussy about being conscious. My whole body was a raw red lump from the salt water and the exposure. There was no feeling in my legs below the knees and my hands wouldn't grip anything. The next big wave would take me off.

And worse than anything else was the pitch, pitch, pitch of the waves. I'd roll with them until I got rolling even farther than they did, and then I'd fall over on my face and be sick. I had nothing to be sick with. I hadn't eaten for two days. But I was sick all the same, in a way that seemed to be tearing my entrails into little shreds and rocketing them out my mouth.

At that point I woke up, and as I woke I told myself I'd kill the Reverend White if I ever saw him again, for making me live through that rubber raft trip one more time.

Then I began to almost wish I was back on the raft. At least I hadn't had a headache in the dream.

My head felt like Goliath's after David was through with him. It felt as if all the inmates of a Federal pen were breaking all the rock for the Trans-Canada highway on my skull. Then I sat up. Jet planes began to fly in the window, through my head and back out the window again. Somewhere just back of my left ear a neurosurgeon was performing a major operation with a dull chisel and no anesthetic.

Anyway, it was a nice bed in a nice room. A nice, light room with morning sunlight flooding it. I saw that much before I had to close my eyes and lie down again.

I was in a wide bed with clean, smooth sheets. I had been undressed and sheathed in pyjamas and put to bed properly with the covers pulled up over me. I opened one eye and a chocolate-brown-painted wall stared at me. It was a little dark, but when I looked farther I could see the other walls of the room were a lively yellow color. The gene-ral effect was good. Besides the bed there were three or four prints on the wall of the room, a high chest of drawers in light wood and modern design, a very thick rug of a light fawn color. I pried the other eye open and that gave me a straight, light-wood bedside table with a double gooseneck on it and a clothes closet door.

I sat up again and this time to anchor myself I swung my legs out of the bed and planted my feet on the floor. That was when I screamed. It wasn't a large scream, nothing that would do justice to the heroine of a mystery movie, but I meant it. I felt as though my leg had split open.

I pulled down the pyjama pants and looked at it, and it had. The cut wasn't as deep as a grave, but it wasn't something you'd hold together with adhesive tape. It was a nice, clean slice. I guess Bing didn't use his razor to shave with, because it wasn't infected.

The bedroom door was open and I could see the

beginning of a hallway from my bed. Holding my head in one hand and my leg in the other I started for the door. I limped like a dance instructor after a hard evening, but I made it. I went down the corridor and came to a sunny living room. It was a nice room, a room to live in rather than to entertain in; most of the furniture was built around the walls and consisted or shelves of cabinets. In them was everything from books to booze. There were four or five isolated radio-chassis that added up to a very high-fidelity radio and record player. There were piles of old magazines that someone had thought worth saving. There was a carved wooden chessboard with the men set in position on one of the cabinets. One door of a well-stocked cellarette was open, in a corner.

An open fireplace of light yellow brick was in the center of one wall, and at the far end of the room French doors opened on a wide terrace. Beyond the terrace you could see the wooded slopes of Mount Royal. The floor of the room was swathed in a soft, heavy Indian rug of dark velvet green. The fireplace wall was painted dark green and matched the rug exactly, and the other walls were pale green. There were three or four pictures, oils, on the walls. There was a chesterfield suite, in pale green.

It was a nice room. I liked it. It was a good thing I did, because it was my own living room, in my own apartment. The boys had taken good care of me. They'd brought me home to bed.

Someone was talking, in the entry just outside the living room door. Probably talking on the telephone, I deduced brightly, since that was where the telephone was. I couldn't quite hear what was being said, but I wasn't really interested. It was my apartment and I knew my way to the kitchen, and that was where I was going.

The coffeepot was sitting on the stove and there was

coffee in it. It had been there for three days but it didn't smell too rancid, so I lit the gas under it. Then I went to the refrigerator. Twelve little stubby pints of Labatt's best were sitting there on the top shelf, where you should keep milk, lined up like soldiers. I selected the closest one. I had strength enough to open it but I couldn't reach up for a glass, so I just brought the bottle back with me to the living room. I collapsed on the chesterfield.

The conversation in the entry stopped about then and the phone clicked back in its cradle. Then Inspector Dorset came in and planted himself on my green rug.

He looked at me sourly. I looked at him sourly.

"Don't argue with me," I said, striking the first blow. "Go find the bathroom. In the medicine cabinet are some small red capsules loaded to the hilt with codeine. Bring me one. That's doctor's orders."

Dorset wasn't usually docile, but maybe I looked as awful as I felt. He brought me the capsule and I washed it down with beer. I leaned back and held my head.

Dorset sat on the edge of one of my light green chairs and waited for me to come around. I couldn't look at him, because I couldn't stomach the color of the chair. I made a mental note to have the furniture reupholstered. The room was way too green for mornings like this.

Dorset cleared his throat. "Where is it?"

"Where is what?" I snapped. I could cope with riddles just then about like Abel coped with Cain.

Dorset sighed. "The notebook," he said. "The little black notebook you took out of the Senator's pocket."

I'd forgotten all about the notebook. I hadn't even looked at it. It was still in my jacket pocket, where I slipped it after the Senator died on the plane, and I told him so.

He shook his head.

"I've looked through all your clothes," he said.

A light began to flicker in my hammering head. "Ha!" I growled. "I suppose that's why I was hijacked."

Dorset sat quietly at the edge of the chair with half his weight on his broad fundament and half on his feet. He looked uncomfortable. His facial expression was uncomfortable, too, as though he had an unpleasant task. I suspected the task was to give me hell for stealing the book.

"Look," I alibied, "I'd forgotten all about that book. I didn't take it from Kelloway's pocket. It was in his hand and when I laid out his body neat in the chair I took it to keep it safe. I would have given it to you last night – at three a.m., I mean – if I'd gone in to see you then."

"You were supposed to come see me, Mr. Teed," Dorset said chidingly. "What happened to you? You'd better start with why you didn't arrive and carry on from there."

"I was waylaid by a blonde girl in a blonde convertible. Maybe you saw her."

"Carol Kelloway."

"That's her," I said. "The Bitch of Endor, if you will forgive me. She whisked me away to talk to me. She took me to the Caravan where, by coincidence of course, three dark drips happened on me. They held me up with a razor and made me drink a Mickey. What makes you see deep purple?"

"I don't know, I'm sure," Dorset said, a bit impatiently. "Stick to the point."

"I saw deep purple. Waves of it. I also saw the Reverend Horatio White, who had apparently hired these razor-honers. I wish I knew who hired him. Maybe it was Carol."

"What was it all about?"

"Horatio was annoyed with me because I gave his name to the *Clarion* – on the passenger list. He claimed he hauled me in just to scare me some. Now I think it over, I suppose he wanted the book."

Dorset said bitterly, "I wish you dough-headed amateurs wouldn't get tangled up in these things."

"I'm not an amateur," I said hotly. "I'm a licensed private investigator."

"I should have your license suspended for withholding evidence," he grunted. "You're a fumbling idiot, you know."

"What was so precious about the notebook?"

"It would tell us why Kelloway made that trip to New York. Willcot said it was the only personal record the Senator kept. And no one knows the reason for his trip."

"Why do you care why he went to New York?" I yapped. "Your case is closed. Carol told me you found no weapon. Forget about the notebook. I'm willing to."

"I'm not," Dorset said pleasantly. "There was something peculiar about that trip, and I'd like to know what it was. Also, whether or not the Senator was murdered, the disappearance of the notebook is theft."

"Surely the R.C.M.P. isn't interested in a simple little case of theft."

"There may be more to it than that," he said. "There may be a lot more. Please get dressed, Mr. Teed. I want you to come down to headquarters with me."

"It will take me an hour," I informed him. "I have a head which needs three cups of coffee and a leg that has to be put back together. You go ahead. I promise to come."

He looked at me doubtfully. He promised an armed guard if I wasn't in his office by noon. Then he trundled out.

By now my leg was hurting worse than my head. I pulled down the pyjama pants and looked at it again. It needed a doctor with some needle and catgut. I called Danny Moore. He took medicine at McGill when I was there and I use him instead of a doctor. I told him what to pack in his black bag.

I didn't have the heart to drink my beer. I took it out to the kitchen, poured it into the frying pan and broiled two thick slices of ham in it. I ate them with my fingers when they were cool enough, and drank three cups of coffee. It wasn't as bad as you'd expect after three days. Danny came.

Danny was about a foot shorter than me, pudgy and cheerful and squeaky clean. He looked pink and healthy as a new mother. He was whistling, but I stopped that.

"Treat me with kid gloves," I said. "I may develop into your best customer."

"You off on another one?" he asked me.

"Could be."

"I'm going to make you up a first-aid kit to carry around. You should have disinfected this."

"It's all right," I said. "I had disinfectant in my veins last night, mixed with my blood."

"It was a sharp knife."

I corrected him. "It was a sharp razor."

He jabbed a needle of local anaesthetic into the skin in a few places and sewed me up. I didn't feel a thing.

"I wish you could shoot some of that into my head," I said sadly. "I have a head condition that has probably never been found before, except by postmortem."

"I've told you before you should cut down on the beer drinking."

"I should cut out the kind of beer I drank last night. It was loaded. I wonder what it was loaded with? Chloral hydrate is the old traditional Mickey. But does it make you see purple?"

"I never heard of anyone seeing purple," Danny said. "Anyhow, chlorol hydrate wouldn't give you a lump on the head. Did you know you had a lumpy head?"

"No, of course not," I said bitterly. "Tell me, won't

you? They hit me. That was after the Mickey."

Danny put away the needlework kit and washed his hands. I had a bandage on my leg big enough to choke a pair of plus-fours. But now I could probably walk without the leg bending in another place as well as at the knee.

Danny said, very casually, from the sink, "I'm by way of being an old friend, confidante and repairman. Right?"

"Sure, if you don't push it." I felt pretty mean.

"Is it all right if I stick my nose in your business for a minute or two?"

"To tell me I'm a stupid bastard, I suppose."

"We graduated from the university together, didn't we? And both spent four years in the Army. Then we both started to build up businesses. I stuck around a hospital picking up a specialist training. You worked on the *Clarion* for a while, and then in a couple of big firms. You got yourself enough know-how on how crooks operated, and how businesses operated, to set up as an investigator, an investigating consultant to big firms. I got the technique to set up as a plastic surgeon. Each of us claimed to be doing what he wanted."

"Okay, come to the point."

"I got a call the other day from one of our better-known mugs here. He happened to be wanted. He wondered if I could kind of play around with his face a bit, so he wouldn't be so easy to recognize when he came out from under his rock again. He offered me ten thousand simoleons to fix him. So I did it, of course."

I sat and looked at him. I was a little slow, but I could excuse myself for that, that morning. I thought it over. I got up and got a pint of beer and a glass and I sat and looked at him some more while I drank it. That didn't make me look at him long enough to embarrass him.

"Forgive me if I think out loud," I said. "But you are

implying you didn't really carve up the crook. You are telling me nicely that I am sticking my neck out."

"I didn't mean to be so damn nice."

"Go on. You make me feel sick, but go on."

"If I got tangled up with crooks, in my business, two things would happen. All the decent business would taper off and, sooner or later, a crook would probably shoot me through the head so nobody alive would know his new face."

"You think I'm setting myself up for a hole in the head?"

"Maybe I could put it across better writing you a letter."

"I'm not tangled up with crooks. They're tangled up with me. And categorically, I've never helped a crook and I never will. That make you love me again?"

"A few months ago I filled up a two-inch hole in your arm. It couldn't have come from anything much smaller than an elephant gun. Then you called me in to dig a slug out of one of your clients. This morning you need me for a gashed leg, a bruised skull and a chloral hangover. What in hell do you think you're doing? If it isn't illegal, all right. But you're still throwing away your career, getting yourself maimed and living a few hair-triggers this side of bloody death. Your business has decayed pretty badly, Son. Nobody outside a padded cell would take risks like this without reasons. Have you got reasons? Are you still doing jobs you want to, for some crazy motive? Or have you just slid into this? If you have, please let me slap you out of it. I could put you in a nice private mental home for a few months. I think I will. I'll try to find you one where they have a few good chess players in other cells."

I sighed. "I suppose this calls for a speech. This isn't much of a morning for a speech. Get two more beers out of the fridg. Get yourself a glass. Sit down."

He wouldn't drink in the morning, but he humored my thirst.

"It's hard to talk about this without sounding phoney. You get hard-boiled enough, you can't talk about anything important without being out of character."

I took a swig of my beer and tried. "I got into this by accident, sort of. The last case, when I got beaten up and shot, I got into that by accident too. So I suppose I did sort of drift into this kind of thing. You're right that far. But if I didn't like it, I'd drift out again. I'm not going around with my eyes sewed shut, and I know what I'm doing. After this thing is over I won't be a business consultant any more, I suppose. Or after the next one, anyhow. I'll lose all that business. I'll be a private eye in the popular meaning of the term. A guy who absorbs any amount of punishment, uses any means for the end of solving his case, never talks straight out of the center of his mouth, and appreciates love enough to take it where it presents itself."

"Glamor," Danny said. "Ah, glamor. That's it, is it? The Army didn't grow you up. You fancy yourself. You fancy yourself, like Walter Mitty. Remember Mitty?"

"Don't try to teach me my Thurber," I said peevishly. "Sure, there's some Mitty in everyone. There's some in every doctor who wants to be a surgeon ... Look, life in the Army was pretty bloody. But you could think of it as glamorous, couldn't you? And you didn't have to persuade yourself too hard you were doing a necessary job. Killing the King's enemies. All right, I'm still doing the same thing. Killing the King's enemies. On a little more personal scale. You want my score, from the last case? One large-scale thug and one doper killed, two dopers arrested, and a murderer that went out and jumped in the broad St. Lawrence."

"Now you're boasting."

"You know what I got this time? Murder, and blackmail. Dirty things, aren't they? Done by dirty people. And I aim to round up those people. What's wrong with that?"

"Take it easy, Hemingway. What's wrong with the police?"

"Enough people like you and me don't help them."

"I'd like to ask a few of your cop friends how much help you are."

"All right. That does it. Can it." I said. "You're as hard on my ideals as I am on MacArnold when he tries to tell me how wonderful it is to be a novelist. Live and let live, will you? I don't mind your wanting to be a doctor."

"What do you mean, murder and blackmail?"

"You always expect to be taken into my confidence."

"I always am."

"All right. Remember your Hippocratic oath. This is as sacred as the confessional. A little under thirty years ago, here in Montreal, a man was implicated in the creation of a bastard. You follow me?"

"I'm trying to."

"The mother in the case got a blackmail threat from the father, a few days ago. I was called in to identify the father, since in spite of everything the mother was too loyal to give him away. Sounds fairly innocent so far, doesn't it?"

"Not too bad. Depending on the people involved."

"They were pretty high class. Not professional crooks. Well. I caught a plane on which the father was guaranteed to be a passenger. There were three men who might have been the father. And one was killed on the trip."

"Because he was the father?"

"I don't even know that. Besides which, I can't get the cops to admit he was murdered."

"What happened?"

"I found him with a knock on his temple. It was a rough night, but he was safety-belted tight into his seat. He died in a matter of minutes."

"What's the police theory? That he got up, fell in the aisle, then belted himself back in before he passed out?"

"Sure. What's the medical verdict on that?"

"Perfectly possible."

"You're a hell of a lot of use."

He scowled. "I could tell a lot more by seeing him. It strikes me there aren't many straight edges in a plane cabin that are sharp enough to smash bone. Describe the wound."

"There aren't any sharp edges," I said. "There aren't any, on purpose. The wound was just in front to the ear and on a level with the top of the ear. It was only a purple bruise, say half-an-inch wide and an inch or so long. But it killed him."

"Ha," Danny exclaimed. I thought for a minute he had something, but he lapsed into deep though. There was always that foolish, vacant look on his face when he was thinking.

He came out. "I'll earn my fee," he said.

"For about the first time."

"Somebody hit him. I'll give you three reasons."

"And I'll give them to Inspector Dorset," I said. "Well?"

"The particular spot you describe is where an artery passes up through a thin channel in the bone to feed the brain. Feel that spot on your own head. Feel a pulse there? Sure. A strong blow just there has this effect: it shatters the bone and ruptures that artery. It doesn't cause concussion or much shock, because the bone is fragile and thin. But as soon as the blood backs up into the brain you've got a kind of cerebral haemorrhage. And that's it."

"Fine," I said. "That's what happened to him. Why didn't he fall? Why do you know he was hit?"

"Provided that's what actually happened," Danny said, "first, it was no accident. Your skull bulges out above that spot and your cheekbone juts out below it, and you could hit it by accident about as easily as you could accidentally thread a needle in the dark. Second, for the same anatomical reasons, nothing he could fall on would hit that spot. You'd have to fall on top of a spiked iron fence to sock it. Third, he would have about one chance in ten thousand of regaining enough consciousness to get back in his seat, let alone buckle his belt."

"I love you forever," I told him, kissing him on both cheeks. I felt exuberant. My head was better and he had fixed me so I could walk, and I was going to walk right to Dorset and tell him what he'd missed.

"Please. I'm a married man. And you smell of beer and God knows what else." He wiped his cheeks off with the back of his hand. "You haven't told me how the rough stuff happened."

"It probably hasn't even got any connection. A character on the plane hated having his name published, so he threw a scare into me."

"Oh, I see," Danny said.

But, when I come to think of it, what about the notebook?

Scene Ten

MOST PEOPLE DON'T KNOW how to shift gears.

You take these great, over-engined, chrome-bedizened American monstrosities of cars – they can be driven by babies and cripples. They don't really need gears at all because the engines work at the same efficiency all the time – about fifty percent of potential. But as if it wasn't enough to power them with engines that, provided they were just built like engines and not like dollar alarm clocks, would lift them right off the ground, they now have gears that change themselves. To someone who likes to drive a car, that's about as sensible as a machine for making babies would be to anyone who likes to manufacture them naturally.

My Riley is different. My Riley takes a delicate hand on the gear lever, like a good jockey's grip on a racehorse's reins. And the results are about the same. About the time I'm going fifty, when I'm just ready to shift into high, I can look in the rear-view mirror and the American cars that got away from the stop light the same time I did are a blur in the distance.

The Riley is a black roadster, seating two. It's low as a lizard, offers about as much air resistance as a telephone wire, and snorts at you, insulted, if you slow for a curve. I'd tell you how much I love it if I could, but the feeling of a car-lover for his machine is as inarticulate as the feeling of a Newfoundlander for rum: you just have to sense it.

I went down to my garage in the basement. I was in a hurry, but not too hurried to not dust Riley off. Then I purred him out of the drive and coasted down Cote des Neiges to Atwater, down Atwater to St. Catherine's, and around the corner to R.C.M.P. headquarters.

It was a beautiful, sunny day. The sky was pale blue without even a hint of mauve, the beer and codeine had tidied up my headache; I wasn't hungry, but at least I was thirsty. That was fairly normal, for me.

I identified my way past the guard at the door and limped toward the back of the building, following the numbers on the doors toward the one he'd given me as Dorset's. I got to it. I knocked and went in.

It was a pleasant, roomy office, newly decorated – the R.C.M.P. had taken over the building only a few years before – with pale green walls that gave it a feeling of spaciousness and height. There was a wide, high window and Dorset's old golden oak desk was placed sideways to that. He had a swivel chair. Beside that there were four straight-backed wooden chairs and three R.C.M.P. constables in the room.

The three constables were introduced to me as Parsons, Collops and Winter. Winter said they had seen me at the airport, where they'd been the three who met the plane with Dorset. I was clearly interrupting something, so I came crookedly over to a chair, favoring my bad, bandaged leg, and sprawled.

"All right," Dorset said. "I want to go over this thing as an integrated story, right from the beginning. Mr. Teed may have something to add. He has been of a little assistance so far. And a little bother."

"Bawl me out in private," I said sensitively. "Your superiors do that much for you when you make mistakes."

He ignored me and concentrated on a page of notes. "After the plane landed it turned at the end of the runway and taxied back to a position in front of the hangar, a few hundred yards north of the passenger terminal building. You lads wheeled the stairway over to the passenger exit of the plane, and I went up and opened the door."

The three constables nodded in unison. They were sitting in the chairs around the office, but they were sitting rigidly, at attention. They had taken off their flat-brimmed bushman's hats. Reflected light glanced off the highly-polished brass of their tunics. The tunics, since they were working constables and not tourist-bait, were olive drab rather than scarlet.

They wore uncomfortably tight riding breeches of navy blue. That was sillier than hell, because all they did was ride around in cars all day.

"I spoke to Mr. Teed. I went inside the cabin and looked at the body. Then Mr. Teed and I came out and walked across to the terminal. The ambulance attendants removed the Senator's body. Then two of you escorted the passengers and the three crew members to the Customs waiting room. Who stayed with the plane?"

Collops and Winter looked at Constable Parsons, who seemed to be the senior. "I did, Sir," he said immediately.

"Did you watch the airline employees unload the luggage from the plane?" I asked him.

"That's what he was there for," Dorset said tersely.

"Yes, I did," Parsons said. "That is, I watched them from inside the cabin. And I didn't let anyone come in the cabin."

"I'll ask the questions," Dorset told me. All cold and efficient with me, he was. "All right. I came back to the Customs room and began interviewing the passengers one by one. I interviewed Mr. Willcot first, so he could go break the news to the Kelloway family. After I interviewed them they were taken over by the Customs and given a strip-search. Meanwhile their luggage had also been searched."

"Willcot didn't get through without a search, did he?" I wanted to know. This time I asked Dorset so he couldn't kick.

"He did not."

Parsons cleared his throat. He looked at me with a fishy eye. "I didn't see Mr. Teed come back to the Customs waiting room after you talked with him, Sir," he suggested.

"Oh, he was searched," Dorset assured him. "They didn't find any deadly weapons. They were a little curious to know why he was carrying three cigarette lighters. And matches too."

"I showed them the Boy Scout motto tattooed on my chest. They took that for an explanation."

"I hope they took the lighters too. Well, I believe there was absolutely nothing of interest revealed by the search."

Winter snickered. Everyone looked at him and he had to say something. "This man LaRouche. Under his pants he was wearing lingerie. Four pairs of ladies' pants. And a slip, with lovely lace. He was embarrassed. Claimed his wife made him do it."

"All right, that's enough trivia," Dorset said sharply over the laughter. "I think we've covered it. Clear out and I'll finish up with Mr. Teed. Tell me when Miss Malone comes."

The three constables filed from the room.

I sat up and took notice. "You didn't tell me Maida Malone was coming. I'd have been here sooner. And more eager."

"You have been eager enough to suit me. I suppose you still have this murder idea on your mind?"

"Don't tell me they're putting on pressure, trying to make you hush it up? You know it was murder."

"There was no weapon. Not in the plane cabin, nor in the luggage, nor on the persons of the passengers and crew. Nor even on the tarmac, where one of them might have ditched it, because we went over that under the floodlights."

"There may not have been a weapon. But he was hit."

"Yes," Dorset agreed. He closed his eyes wearily and brushed his wispy, dry hair back from his weathered forehead. "Yes, he was hit, Mr. Teed. And you were attacked because you had his notebook. And we have only hints of what it was all about."

"I'm glad you have hints. I haven't any more idea about it than I have who killed Edwin Drood." Dorset looked puzzled. "That was the murder mystery Charles Dickens started to write and forgot to solve."

"Oh. And how do you know he was hit?"

"I found him. And I've been talking to a doctor."

"Don't talk too much. Don't talk to any newspapers, or I'll throw you in a cell right now."

"If I promise, will you tell me your hints?"

"No," he said definitely. "You answer my questions."

He made me go all through the plane trip again, beginning at LaGuardia and filling in every detail. The only thing I skipped was the little scene between Willcot and Lorette Toledo before the trip began. I figured Willcot was clear anyway.

After I got through he thumbed over his notes again. "What about the monkey business getting on the plane?"

"Oh. With Willcot?"

"Yes. He's still mad at you."

"I don't care if he is."

"You were a little too smart, trying to pump him and get his reaction when you told him the Senator was dead. He thinks you did it."

"Do you think so?"

"There were twelve people on that plane – after the Senator was killed. One of you did it. Only Willcot had an obvious connection with the Senator, and I haven't found any motive for him yet. So I have to probe the other eleven.

I'll start with you. Had you ever met the Senator before?"

"No."

"Why did you want to sit next to him?"

"I wanted to meet him."

"Don't clown, Mr. Teed. I'm not."

His telephone buzzed. He answered it and said, "All right. Ask her to wait." He nodded for me to go on.

"I was working on a case. I wanted to ask the Senator some questions. It couldn't have had anything to do with his death," I said. I crossed my fingers, though.

"You'll talk later if you don't talk now," Dorset grumped wearily. "Did you have anything against the Senator?"

"Only my Communist convictions."

"Oh, get out of here and let me think. One thing. If anyone approaches you in any way about that notebook, get in touch with me. Get in touch with me before you do anything else."

I nodded. "About the weapon," I said. "I wonder if there was anything in the galley – you know, the little cubbyhole where Maida did her cooking?"

"I intend to ask her," he said with dignity.

"Can I stay around and listen?"

"Good afternoon, Mr. Teed."

It was afternoon, at that. I don't know where they had hidden Maida. I looked for her on my way out, but she was behind a door somewhere. I needed lunch. I got in Riley and steamed off to the Peel Tavern and drank a substantial lunch, with a Western sandwich on the side. I came back and parked across the street from R.C.M.P. headquarters, in case Maida was still inside. After a while, she came out. I was in luck. She crossed the street toward Riley and me.

She was in civvies. She wore a royal blue and light-blue striped dress of some limp, silky material. And she was really designed to wear a limp dress. It clung to a figure you couldn't quite believe. She was a tall girl and her height was all in her long, sweeping legs. From the waist up her body had the lines of a Greek statue – and I don't mean the Discus Thrower. The blue dress made her eyes deep blue; blue eyes, black hair, lovely fair skin.

I didn't need to speak to her because there wasn't really anything I wanted to ask her about the case. I wasn't interested in the case any more. I wanted to devote the rest of the year to her.

"Maida!"

The black curls tossed as she turned her head.

"Could I give you a lift?"

She came closer. She smiled. "It's Mr. Teed."

"It's Russ," I corrected.

"Thank you." I opened the door and she got in.

I started Riley. She was looking at me. She waited to speak until we stopped for a red light and I could look back. "Please," she said, with the sad Irish music in her voice. "Don't talk about the poor Senator. I've just been all through it again. The awful trip."

"Let's forget it. Come with me. I know a bar called the Trafalgar where they make the best forgetting potions in the city."

"I'm afraid I'll have to go right home. Mother's waiting for me. But you can come in for a drink, if you will."

She said it very prettily. She probably had nothing at home but a dusty old bottle of gin with nothing to mix in it, but she could make any kind of martyr she wanted of me. We were going west on St. Catherine. "Wonderful," I said. "Where's home?"

"I have an apartment on Shuter Street."

We slid and sideswiped through the mid-afternoon

traffic on St. Catherine, turned up University, where it said No Left Turn but there wasn't a cop, took Milton to Shuter and came to rest in front of a plain old greystone house full of one- and two-room apartments. She had one large room on the first floor front, and I felt sorry for her because it was clearly a furnished apartment and only tasteless, color-blind people should live in furnished apartments.

She called, "Mother!" as soon as we came in. She looked embarrassed when she got no answer. "I suppose mother was delayed shopping," she explained. Then she opened a door to a small, airless closet fixed up as a kitchen and made me reach for a bottle of very reasonable rye and mix our drinks.

I came back to the chesterfield with them and perched beside her. "How long have you been a hostess?" I asked her.

"Three years."

"Like it?"

She made a little face. "Pretty well"

"You took nursing before that?"

She nodded.

"Where was that?"

"Here in Montreal."

"Montreal your home?"

She nodded again.

"And your mother," I asked. "Was she frightened by a deaf-mute, just before you were born?"

She had been worrying, worrying hard about something and paying no attention at all to me. There was a look in her eyes that went right through me. There was a look in my eyes, incidentally, that went right into the depths of her lovely ones and got lost there.

But I'd knocked her out of it. The question wasn't routine enough to answer automatically. She stared at me still but she gradually began to see me again, and then she got it and laughed. She stood up and bent and kissed me lightly on the cheek. "Oh, I'm sorry," she said. "I was worrying about mother. She was so anxious for me to be here, and she's late. But you see, I can't resist you. Make love to me quickly before she comes back." She went across the room and turned on the radio. She looked casually but anxiously out the window onto the street, on her way.

She came back and was going to sit down, but I forestalled that. I set my drink carefully on a table and stood up and showed her that kisses were something you didn't fool with. It was something I'd been wanting to do since before the Senator died.

When we broke apart she had that wide, quiet look in her eyes and her face was happy and a little amazed. I don't know how I looked, but the way I felt was something far beyond kisses and much deeper in the night.

"I ... " She stopped and smiled. It was a delicious smile. "I don't know you, Mr. Teed."

"Russ. Come see my apartment. It's my best reference."

"Certainly not," she smiled, "Mr. Teed."

The door began to open. I just had time to detach my hands and make them straighten my tie.

"Hello, Mother."

Mother was an Irish beauty too, older but not faded. She was a slight little woman and her gay black hair had been a little tamed and greyed by time. Her face was smooth and its flesh firm. Her eyes were even more striking than Maida's; they were as deep and as wide, but a restless, burning black. She wore a quiet, neat tailored grey suit and a blouse plain and fresh as wildflowers.

"Mother, this is Mr. Teed."

I collected myself. "How do you do, Mrs. Malone."

She gave me a courtly nod. "How do you do, Mr. Teed.

Not Mrs. Malone. Miss Malone."

I could feel my lower teeth sinking away from my uppers as my jaw went limp. I probably looked silly as hell. "Mother of God," I said with all due reverence. "Another one!"

"I beg your pardon?" she asked politely.

"Another ba—Oh, no," I said. "Please. Let me begin all over again. I was forgetting myself."

Maida gathered what was wrong, or at least part of what was wrong. She laughed. She had a lovely laugh, but it didn't help my discomfort.

"It's quite all right, Mr. Teed. Don't be shocked. My mother insists on using her maiden name."

"Of course," I said. "Naturally. Now, now, I didn't ..."

At this point Miss Malone, mère, was also laughing.

"There are certain good enough reasons, Mr. Teed, why my former husband's name is never mentioned."

"Oh," I said vaguely. "Yes. Now, if you would pardon me, Mrs. ... Miss Malone, I'm afraid I must be leaving." I smiled. I gave her a very nice little bow and walked smartly through the door and into the closet they used for a kitchen.

When I got out again I said, "Good-bye, Maida. May I call you? I would like to call you. Mustn't keep you now. Thanks, I'll find the door. Did you hide it over here?"

She found the door for me.

As I navigated through it I could hear Miss Malone, Senior. She was still laughing.

Scene Eleven

TEED, I SAID TO MYSELF sharply and nastily, you are hopelessly drunk. I got into Riley and awkwardly slammed the door on my left foot to prove it. Teed, I said emphatically, you are drunk as a bastard.

Can't we keep that word out of the conversation, please?

Well, can't we keep that angle out of the case? That would be more to the point.

Apparently not out of the female angle of the case. So far we had one redhead who admittedly didn't know her own father, and one brunette who had disowned hers if he was known. At least we had Carol, a blonde who was presumptively legitimate. Presumably legitimate. No, presumptively, that was probably a word. To hell with playing with words. Words were troublemakers.

Take the word bastard. A perfectly respectable word with a clear, unequivocal meaning. See, I had words to burn. Unequivocal. I could think it even if my tongue wouldn't say it. In the old days people were proud of being bastards. They put it on their coats of arms. What was wrong with good, honest bastardy?

I had one answer to that one. It sometimes made the location of Father a bit of a detective job. Too bad I wasn't a better detective. I'd like to detect Maida's father. I'd like to detect Maida. Maida I'd like to ...

Riley had arrived. It had been driving itself carefully, minding its own business as it always does when it knows I can't see anything. It knows two places to go at those times: home to its garage, and downtown to my office. Luckily, it had gone to the office. That was where I wanted to go.

My office was in the Canam Building, which is across the street from the Dominion Square Building and next door to the Sun Life, making it almost on Dominion Square. Life is sometimes full of almosts. The Canam was almost as respectable as the Dominion Square and almost as well-appointed as the Sun Life. It was almost as nice a building as I'd wanted and I was almost satisfied with my office in it. Ah, well.

The office was a big one with a solid partition dividing it into reception room and private sanctum. The reception end, being unlighted, was dark as the bars the tourists go to along Peel Street, but this was a delusion. There was no liquor there. The liquor was inside.

I unlocked the reception room door and turned on the lights. They gleamed on the polished mahogany of tabletop and chair backs, shone in soft highlights on blue leather chair seats and sank into deep royal-blue broadloom. This was a small room, but one to make an entering client catch his breath and start figuring how much he could afford to pay me for a case. That was why I'd laid out money on it.

I juggled keys and found the one to the inner office. I went in, turned sharply left, and began operations on a large safe in the corner. I'd taken the office over from a wholesale jeweler and got the safe cheap from him. Painted dark blue to match the room it didn't look too obtrusive, and you never know when a safe was going to be handy. Meanwhile, I locked my valuables in it to keep them away from the charwoman.

My most valuable valuable was right there on the top shelf and when the heavy door clicked open I felt it was just what I needed. I lifted it carefully by its royal purple cap, the beautiful crown-shaped bottle with its load of amber nectar, and cradled in tenderly under one arm while I shut the safe.

"Crown Royal rye, indeed," said a voice behind me. "I'll bet you never open that safe if you know a client's in the office."

I turned around carefully. I'd as soon have been shot as drop the Crown Royal.

My eyes caught a gleam of red gold and a flash of silver. It was the redhead. Smiling.

I was fickle that day. The moment I looked at her, I began to forget Maida Malone. I can't explain why. She didn't have the figure, the face or the eyes. All she had were those two reams of glamorous red hair, and bands. And a look about her that made me want to look after her. Preferably, for a long time.

"This is the way you work on my case!" she said with good-natured scorn.

"Sure."

She was sitting behind my broad mahogany desk. I came toward her, because the glasses were on the desk. I poured drinks, and pulled the glass stopper out of the ice-water thermos jug. I let her water her own drink, and she had the good sense not to drown it.

"I would ask how you got in here," I said, "if I didn't know my janitor so well. He's susceptible."

"And I," she said, a bit nettled, "would ask you how you got that silly smear of lipstick on your mouth, if it were any of my business."

The glib, blasé Teed was a bit of an awkward ass this day. Like a guilty kid caught by mamma after his first date, I whipped out my breast-pocket handkerchief to wipe. With the handkerchief, a small cloud of American hundred-dollar bills popped out and fluttered to the floor. That was just dandy. I stooped to pick them up, and my slit leg started to crack open again and I landed nose-first on my blue broadloom. The only thing I needed to complete the picture was to have my headache come back, and it did, just after my head hit the carpet. I lay there.

The redhead laughed at me.

"Ann," I said gently. There was no more edge to my voice than to a new Gilette blade. "Ann, either hand me my drink or I will get pliers and tighten those bands until your teeth crack."

"You leave my bands alone."

"Give me that drink. And don't laugh at me anymore."

"My, we're tough today. Get your own drink."

I sat up and eyed her just the odd bit balefully. "This suit has two pairs of pants."

"Is that supposed to be a threat?"

"I'm going to tell you how much I've suffered for you. The other pair of pants to this suit has a razor slash four inches long across the leg. And the slash was an inch deeper than the cloth."

Her eyes widened. She looked scared.

"Also, a man was killed on the plane."

She nodded. "Senator Kelloway. I know. That's why I came. I flew up on the noon plane after I saw it in the New York morning papers."

"Why? Was he your daddy?"

She shrugged impatiently. "I don't know. I've told you I have no idea who my father is. I suppose he might have been. If you don't know, I don't."

"I'm not Houdini. There were three men on that plane who might have been your father. I thought Kelloway was the most likely, and I was going to go into the matter with him. Then he got killed. I doubt if that proves anything. I doubt, for instance, that it proves he was your father. Who would want to kill your father ... particularly?"

She bit her lip. She tried not to cry. She was full to the fizz-point of emotions I didn't understand.

"Well?" I said.

"Tell me ... what you've done," she managed.

"Tell me what *you've* done. Have you seen Margaret since you arrived?"

"I ... I telephoned her from here."

"When did she get back from New York?"

That did it. She let the tears go. Somehow, I found enough strength to get off the floor. I came around the desk and lifted her out of the chair and held her where she could get my left shoulder all wet. I couldn't see her face, but the most beautiful red hair in the world rested against my cheek. Her body was slim and cool and tremb--ling in my arms. And you wouldn't believe that small breasts could be so obviously present, firm and thrilling against me.

More than anything else in the world, I wanted to find her father, if that would make things right for her. I'd let him have one look at her, so he could see what a daughter he'd been missing, before I took him out and threw him under an asphalt road-roller.

Then a great light began to dawn in my head. It came on slowly and with flickers at first, on a fluorescent tube.

"Oh, my God!" I said softly. "Ann Wedgewood. Margaret Derby. Royal Crown Derby. Margaret Derby Smythe. Mrs. H. J. Smythe. Oh, my God. Your mother was on that plane!"

She stopped crying in a minute. She tensed, as though she'd just suddenly realized she was in my arms, and shoved back. She dug up a handkerchief the size of a tea bag from somewhere, and blew her nose. It was a red nose, but she was still lovely.

She said, "It was a silly" – sniff – "idea." Sniff. "I don't know whether she thought of it in desperation or humor. Ann Wedgewood, because her name was Derby. It's my legal name now, of course."

"We better get down to brass tacks. What did she slug him with?"

"What?"

"Your mother hit your father. I don't particularly blame her. But what did she hit him with?"

"Don't be ridiculous," she said bitingly.

"Leave us be reasonable," I said, irritated. "What were you crying for?"

"Because the police will be bound to believe that is what happened, when they get the full story. But I certainly didn't think you would."

"It isn't too hard to figure," I protested. "Your late father, the Senator, was a gold-plated heel. He was trying a little refined blackmail on your mother, and she was pretty desperate. During the stormy plane flight she saw her chance and acted on impulse. As I said, I don't blame her."

"Reasoned like a true detective," Ann said bitterly. "All right, starting from that, you've got to find out what actually happened. You've got to prove that just exactly what you said isn't true."

"Maybe it is."

There was a way to see her bands without making her smile. That was to make her so mad she drew back her lips in an enraged grimace. I was finding that out, just then. The bands still looked cute, but that wasn't why she was doing it. She was nearly spitting at me.

"Of all the people in Montreal I could have asked to help me, why did I have to remember your name? Why, you – you rye-sodden excuse for a man, you would probably investigate the parish priest first if you were hired to find who broke open the poor-box. Because he had the most opportunity. Did you ever stop to think that character means something in crime detection? That as well as opportunity and motive, a person must be capable of committing crime? Or are you so sunk in your own peculiar brand of cynicism that you won't admit there are honest, harmless people in the world? People who wouldn't willingly hurt or trespass against anyone, because they've grown up honest people, because that's their character, their whole being. Did you know that? Do you know any people like that?"

"Not many," I said, nettled. But it was a weak stopper.

"I thought I was going to like you, that day in New York. First impressions can be awfully strong, and awfully wrong. I thought you were some very high type of character devoted to helping people in trouble and advancing the cause of justice, and all that rot. Sort of a modern knight-errant. Chivalry is not dead, and all that. And I thought I was through being naive! How starry-eyed can you get, I wonder?"

"Now, wait," I yelled. "So you've got a romantic attitude toward life. So I have too, or I wouldn't be in this business. Especially, I wouldn't be trying to do this job for you. The toughest private eye you can find in a pocket reprint is a romantic at heart."

I stopped and finished my drink in a long gulp and lit a cigarette and then said, "Oh, Ann, why the hell did we get mixed up and start fighting? All we're really after is, did Margaret kill the Senator?"

"But she couldn't! She's the gentlest, sweetest person in the world. She couldn't even raise her hand to strike a blow."

"All right. We'll have to try to figure out what really did happen on the plane. I'll take it on faith that Margaret had nothing to do with it, until I meet her."

"What do you mean, until you meet her?"

"I had a friend once who thought his wife was the most wonderful girl in the world. I thought she was psychotic, but you couldn't tell him that. He kept right on being completely in love with her until the day she strangled their baby because he was crying too loud. All I'm trying to say in my awkward way, is that people appear differently to the various people who meet them."

"Oh, God! What a morbid mind you have! Do you keep a scrapbook of episodes like that to reinforce your cynicism?"

"It's not just cynicism!" I shouted at her. "I fell in love with a girl once, and found out later she'd done murder. I met a kind, merry white-haired little druggist and it developed he supplied all the dope to all the addicts in Montreal. Grow up, will you? People aren't always supplied with a character that mirrors their external works."

"No," she said, and she looked straight at me, and she meant me.

"Sure. People are what they're made. I won't change one bit of me, I won't reform, and I have to tell you all about it. I have to sit here and fight with you and try to tell you how I see things, if it makes you hate me forever. At the same time as I'm maybe falling in love with you. I've got to get my head read. There's a brunette down the street with eyes as old as Eve who thinks I'm wonderful. No, she doesn't think about it at all, she just knows it. There's a blonde up the hill with curves that make you look straight as the Queen Elizabeth Way. And I have to fall for a set of bands and a few waves of carroty hair."

I had said my piece. I poured more Crown Royal. For myself. Much more. I started working on it, without water.

She stood up. She said, "I think I fell a little bit in love with you, too, that first day in New York. You're dark and tall and clean-cut and romantic. More like someone in a good play than in a movie, because you seemed to be ... oh, intelligent and understanding. But the intelligence is just a sharp, surface brightness and the understanding is just a willingness to believe people capable of anything bad. You specialize in hurting and being hurt, don't you? You want to be so precious frank and honest, no matter who it hurts. No matter how much it hurts you. You sadist! You masochist! You ... you private eye!"

She was going to cry again, but this time she didn't want a shoulder to cry on. Anyway, not my shoulder. She walked stiffly past me and out of my office. The sun went in. It started to rain. The supreme tragedy of it all was that Riley was out on the street with his top down.

I went sadly to the street and put up Riley's top so he wouldn't get any wetter. Then I hailed a taxi to take me to see MacArnold.

I felt so sad I made the taxi wait for me outside the Mount Royal while I went into the Pic and had one more bracer.

Scene Twelve

On Shuter Street, not too far from the Misses Malone, was a very old greystone house come far enough down in the world to let out apartments to newsmen. In one of the dirtier of these apartments lived MacArnold, reporter for the *Clarion* until that day in the near future when they would fire him for drunkenness, a man with much more intelligence than sense, more ambition than accomplishment, and more ideals than energy. He followed an invariable routine of working evenings on the paper, drinking until shortly before breakfast, sleeping until his hangover woke him up, and working on novels until it was time to go back to the *Clarion*. The novels he wrote concerned women dying of consumption, hopelessly in love with heroes about to be unjustly hanged. They sounded like he'd written them during a hangover, all right. An opium hangover.

It was early afternoon, and I got there before MacArnold woke up. There was a quart of milk slowly going sour at his door. I picked it up and took a swig and it was still all right, but it was homogenized and the cream hadn't risen to the top so I put the top back on. I beat on his door. There was no response. I tried a more direct approach, and it wasn't locked, so I walked in.

MacArnold, a dull film over his eyes, stared at me coldly from his untidy day bed. "There is beer in the icebox," he said. "There are three quarts. You can drink them all if you'll just let me sleep and go away quietly. That is how much I hate you."

I went to the closet he called kitchen. I started on one of the beers and put the coffeepot on his gas burner. When it began boiling the fumes got him out of bed and out there.

He looked at the beer and shuddered. "Alcoholic!" he grunted.

"I am not an alcoholic," I pointed out. "I am a heavy drinker. There's a difference. An alcoholic is a drinker who lets liquor interfere with his life. Alcohol just improves mine."

"An alcoholic is someone with an uncontrollable urge to drink all the time. Like you."

"It's not uncontrollable. There just isn't any need to control it at times like this." I swigged the beer.

"All right. You're not an alcoholic. I'm an alcoholic. What I drank last night is interfering with my desire to live right now." He went into the bathroom.

"What do you take from those hypodermics to pull you back together?"

"Intravenous glucose," he yelled through the door. Then he came out. "The great kidder," he said bitterly. "Can't I brush my teeth and dunk my head without getting ridden? Pour me the coffee. And you'd better have some too."

"Why so bitter? I told Hatch to give you the byline on that story I wrote last night. Didn't he?"

"Of course not."

"Well, let's make it into enough of a story to rate one. The Senator is murdered, all right, and officially, but not for publication. Want to help me work on some other angles?"

He wanted to know about the angles. I told him the whole story, beginning with Ann's phone call that took me through the night to New York and not skipping anything except a few last names. You can trust a newsman with an off-the-record story, if you don't tell him last names.

"I thought you'd like to know all about it before we start," I said.

"Yeah."

"Well. Got any ideas?"

"No."

"Seen Carol lately?"

"You slob, did you come here to have me help you with a case or to horse around with me?"

"Relax. I just asked."

"You know goddamned well I haven't seen Carol. Not for two years. You know I wouldn't have a hangover this morning if I'd seen Carol. Nor any other morning."

"I doubt that, but skip it. All right. So that's one reason I brought you into this. Carol's tied up in it. You know Carol."

He corrected me. "I knew Carol."

"What's she like?"

"The beautiful, blonde Kelloway? Like any other girl a guy falls in love with, and finds she won't love back. Maybe she can't love back, I don't know. I should throw you out of here for making me remember. But what the hell, I'd kid myself if I thought I'd forgotten the way she crooked her little finger."

"Here's the point," I said. "Carol took me to the Caravan Club. She was driving. It wasn't my idea. So after she leaves, these three jumped-up fancy boys come in and lead me away by the nose. Or by the leg. So whose idea was that?"

"From the way you tell it, it was the Reverend White's idea."

"Yes, but who calls his tune? He's no independent operator. I'll stake on that."

"You said this guy Scarper and his show-girl were there. They could have seen you come in and then one of them slipped off and called White. That might have been it."

"Whoever it was wanted the little notebook I took

from Kelloway's body. That could be Scarper, though I don't know why. There's a good reason why it could have been Carol. If the Senator was doing something out of line in New York, it would be in that book. And she knew what he was in New York for, she said. So she had the book stolen to avoid the publicity."

"How did she know you had it?"

"How did anybody know I had it? Except Dorset – he guessed. Willcot, the secretary, told him about the book and Dorset knew I'd been over the body."

"Maybe – no, I don't know."

"Would Carol have me laid out to get that book back?"

"If you had an old postage stamp that Carol wanted, she'd lay you out to get it back. If she couldn't get it any other way."

"You sound bitter."

"Who knows? Maybe I am. But Carol would be likely to work you over with her charms to try and get the book that way first. The slugging would come if that didn't pay off."

"I wasn't in a receptive mood. I think she sensed it. So we can't write it off with that one."

"What we want to find out is more about the Reverend White."

"Just what I was thinking," I agreed.

"All right," he said. "I know where to go. Provided he's crooked. There is one character who knows all about all the crooks in town. I will lead you to him by the hand. That I should be waked up to do this! You could have thought of it yourself."

"Now that you've made yourself feel all superior, will you tell me who you're talking about?"

"Louie Two," he said.

After MacArnold finished his coffee we got another

cab and went to Louis Two's bar. This is an establishment on Dorchester Street run by Louis Two and Louis Three, who are brothers. Louis One, their father, does not enter the picture since he is dead. He starved to death during the Great Depression. Louis Two's is the most logical place in town to go if you are fool enough to want to buy a newsman a drink. It is a good place to keep away from unless you have money to loan or are harder-hearted than Scrooge before he saw his ghosts.

We went into the bar. We walked up the old stone steps of a converted house, which is what most Montreal bars are, into a long room that probably used to be living room and dining room and some of the kitchen and was now very dim and full of little tables and hard chairs. Shining brightly at the end of the room, like a small restaurant at the end of a lonely road, was a big bar backed by gaudy bottles. There were no waiters around and hardly enough customers to pay for lighting the bar.

Louis Three was behind the bar, a very broad type with a kind face and the ears of a boxer. He had been a boxer, and Louis Two had managed him, and he'd never won a fight.

"Greetings," he said.

"Salutations," said MacArnold. "Where's Louis Two?"

"Louis Two," said Louis Three with dignity, "is a character. We allow him to save himself for the tourists, at night. He is sleeping."

"What does it take to wake him up?"

"In a good mood or in a bad mood?"

"In a good mood, by all means," I said.

"It takes a kitten. He hears a little kitten drinking milk and purring beside his bed, he wakes up all smiling."

"Touching," I commented. "Do you keep a kitten for that purpose?"

"We keep milk. That's just as good."

There was a pause while MacArnold went out to the alley and caught a kitten and brought it back. The kitten smelled as though it had been rolling in fish brought from the Indian Sea by slow boat, but when faced with milk it purred. We took the milk and the kitten behind the bar to where Louis Two was sprawled on his cot bed. The kitten purred as close to Louis Two as we could arrange it. Nothing happened. After a few minutes MacArnold started purring in rhythm with the kitten to raise the sound level a few decibels. A beatific smile spread over the face of the sleeping Louis Two.

Louis Two had the grandfather of all the kindly, comic, pathetic faces you ever saw; a little like a billiard-bald Charlie Chaplin. He opened his eyes and then threw back the sheet and sat on the side of his cot. He was a wizened little man in his underwear, with black hair plastered sparsely across clammy white skin on his chest and his pipestem arms and legs. He watched the kitten and his smile broadened across his toothless gums and spread up, wrinkling the corners of the sparkling little eyes. He stroked the kitten. Then he looked up and saw MacArnold.

He tried to say something but it didn't come out recognizable. He reached under the bed and got his teeth and put them in. He said, "Hello, Macky. Hello Russy. What you drinking?"

I said I'd have milk for my ulcer, with a little Scotch in it, and MacArnold wanted beer. Louis Three got them for us. He also gave Louis Two a double orange juice with two ounces of gin, for his breakfast.

"We came to see you because you know all the answers, Louis," MacArnold told him.

He made it sound enough like kidding so Louis Two wouldn't think he was just greasing the ways. "Depends on what you're asking me, Macky. And you too, Russy boy. One thing you want to know, I don't know."

"What's that?"

"I don't know who killed Kelloway."

"Would you mind telling me," I said carefully, "how it is that you know that I would like to know that?"

Louis Two shrugged innocently. "So many people tell me things. Maybe it was Ike Scarper. I kind of think it was."

"Friend of yours?"

"A very, very dear companion," he assured me.

"By the way, what does he do?"

"Why Russy! How would I know? I only meet him in his leisure hours. I think that he kind of likes to come in here for a drink on occasion. He sits around and talks to me. About what, you'd wonder? I'll tell you, Russy. We discuss horses."

That got us about as far as a round trip to the men's room. What he knew about Scarper he wasn't telling, not to me.

"What we really wondered," MacArnold cued in, "was if you knew anything about a black boy named Horatio White."

"Ah," Louis Two said thoughtfully.

"The Reverend Horatio White," I added.

"Ah! Him. That lard-lump. Him, I'd keep clear of, Russy. Not that he is anything to worry about, but he has in employment with him a very smart young boy. I do not know that I remember the name. I get the impression he would slice off your ear if there was an earring in it."

That was my cue to take off my pants and show him my bandage. "I've met the boy," I said simply.

"Bastard!" Louis Two said gently. He hated his friends to get hurt.

"The boy worked me over to get something I was

carrying, something that might tell us why Kelloway was slugged. He got this item for friend Horatio. But where does Horatio fit in? Who does he work for? Or was he maybe just working on his own and bumped the Senator all by himself?"

Louis Two put one hand, palm down and held very flat, to the top of his bald head and polished till it glowed like a silicone wax job. "Horatio is unsavoury," he said definitely. "On the other hand it is my opinion he would not murder anybody. His guts are too soft. He would let the boy do it."

"The boy wasn't on the plane," I said gloomily. "And no one else on the plane would be working for Horatio."

"I will tell you about this minister," Louis Two decided. "This, you will understand, is only what I hear. But I hear it from a number of sources. There was a big mortgage on that church which he preached at. Around twenty grand. It got all paid off."

"I've been told that before," I said. "Horatio himself told me."

"Did he tell you who paid off the mortgage? He did. Did he tell you how? Being minister, he was in a very good spot to know just whom had money in that congregation of his, as some did. So the boy – Petey, the name is – did persuasion where it would do the most good. Petey got the money for Horatio and Horatio paid off the mortgage."

"And that's what you hear?"

"That's what I hear."

"Sounds silly as hell to me," I grunted. "Why didn't he just keep the money, if he went to that much trouble to get it?"

"Two reasons, Russy boy. One was, he got a good cut."

"Which he used to got on a binge in New York. But that wouldn't be as good as keeping the whole bundle."

"He was scared to. First, see, he started this business with Petey. It was bringing him in a very sustaining income, and when those that held the mortgage heard of it, they felt it had become time for the mortgage to be paid off. They told Horatio he better divert funds their way. Or else."

"I see," I said, trying to do a lot of thinking all at once. "I see. And who held the mortgage?"

"A very good question, Russy," Louis Two said. He paused. He cleared his throat. "Have you any other good questions?" he wanted to know.

"Okay," I said. "Thanks, anyway."

"Any time, Russy. Any time. But take better care of yourself."

"Tell Petey to take care of himself," I snorted.

We left the bar.

"How can you get so much out of him?" MacArnold wanted to know. "Does he think you're good protection for him, or what?"

"He's a pretty square egg," I said.

"Yeah. He won't sell heroin to anyone who doesn't really need it."

"He doesn't sell heroin, and you know it. He operates on the thin edge of the law. So do I. We get along all right. I do favors for him too."

"And you wouldn't turn in any of his very, very dear friends, I suppose."

"Not unless I had to."

We came into sight of the Laurentian Hotel. When we got to it, without either of us making a suggestion, we turned in. We went downstairs into the Pine Lounge; MacArnold owed money to so many guys in the Press Club he didn't dare take me there. We sat and ordered beers.

MacArnold pursued the topic. "For instance, in this

matter at hand. I wonder who held that mortgage?"

"It might make mores sense if we found out."

MacArnold picked up his beer glass and took it to a phone booth. After a while he came back, caught another bottle from the waiter and took that into the booth too. He came back finally with the empty bottle and glass.

"Took four calls," he explained. He looked for the waiter.

"Well?"

"Sure it was," he said.

"Ike Scarper."

"Yep."

"Let me train my sights on it for a minute."

I brooded, and we both drank two more beers. MacArnold tried to pick up a blonde but her man came back from where he'd been. I played with the sand in the window boxes and let my mind turn over slowly.

I said, "Suppose the Senator was onto the Scarper-White-Petey racket. He went to New York to get more dope on it."

"You popped a fly into the infield on the first ball."

"Yeah, it's a bit thin. But Horatio was in New York, so maybe the Senator went down there to catch him in a weakened condition and drag it out of him."

"Tell me this: why is a man as big as Kelloway interested in a little twenty-thousand dollar scandal?"

"I can give you that one," I said. "Scarper is a guy we don't know too much about. He was a little soiled around the edges, not above turning the odd thousand by reaming a Negro congregation. But I also have rumors he was a pretty big market shark in some other deals. Say he was annoying the Senator and the Senator wanted to get rid of him. This might be the way to do it, like income tax was the way they got Capone."

"Okay. What else you got?"

"Scarper finds out Kelloway has gone to New York, and guesses why. He heads down there, finds out from Horatio that Kelloway has busted the racket, and catches the same plane back as the Senator. He takes advantage of the bumpy ride to wallop him. The only problem is, I find the notebook, which contains enough notes to break him apart. So he instructs Horatio to have Petey get it from me. He put them onto me when he saw me sitting in the Caravan."

"Could be."

"That lets Carol out, I'm afraid."

"I'm glad."

"Aw, go to hell," I said impatiently.

MacArnold was drunk enough to forget he was a man. "I'd be willing to die next day to sleep with her one night."

"Again, you mean."

"Not again. That was the worst part of it."

"Tell her. She'll let you do it if you promised to let her watch you die. It would be a new thrill."

MacArnold threw the beer out of his glass into my face. Before I could even get my handkerchief out there were three waiters standing around the table. We got up without a word and walked away together.

"I'm sorry," I said.

"So am I."

"Love is a hell of a thing."

"That line's one I wouldn't even put in one of *my* novels."

We walked in silence up Windsor Street toward St. Catherine.

"What do we do now?" MacArnold asked.

"It's dinnertime."

"I suppose Scarper is the next stop."

"No. I don't know where to find him. And it wouldn't do us any good. He has the notebook by now, and he's burnt it. Finding him won't get us anything but bloody heads or hacked-off ears."

"So where do we go?"

"Home for dinner." I steered off to the right across Dominion Square toward Riley.

"And then what?"

"I'm going to go see Carol," I said. "She thought she knew why the Senator went to New York. I'll tell her this story and see if it checks."

We got to Riley and folded ourselves in.

"You want to come?" I asked him.

"Hell, no," he said.

We drove across St. Catherine and up to Sherbrooke and then west on Sherbrooke to Cote des Neiges. The traffic light stopped us there and it was quiet for a minute.

"Hell, yes," he said.

Scene Thirteen

SPAM, SPEEF, SPORK, SPOOF and things like that have been sadly maligned, mainly because too many limeys had to eat too much of them while the war was on. Treated properly, they're fine.

I took a can of Prem and dismantled it and sliced the stuff fairly thin. I got a frying pan hot and laid the slices in it to sear and sizzle and then opened one can of niblets and one of peas. When the Prem was turned once I poured the vegetables in and left them until they were bubbling.

"It's good?" MacArnold said with his face expressing wild unbelief.

"You're a bachelor too. You could do as well."

"I don't have this startling originality of yours."

"You've got anything you can get from me," I said. "You can omit the paeans."

We went through four quarts of Molson – that was only two apiece – doing the dishes. By then, for no apparent reason, it was nine o'clock.

"The Kelloways should be through their dishes also," I said with decision.

"Yeah."

"We will go and talk to Carol."

"Yeah."

"You sound enthusiastic."

"How the hell do you think you'd sound? I don't suppose you've ever been in love. Not the way I was in love with Carol, anyway."

"One thing about this business," I said resignedly, "You have to get used to meeting a lot of philosophy in the course of a day's work. You want to talk about love?"

"To hell with love," he said.

"You got to realize this about love. It hasn't got anything to do with liking, or wanting to live with permanently, or things like that. It's strictly for the lower mammals."

"Thank you for telling me all. Go on being a goddam automaton and I'll live the way I feel like."

"Sure," I said. I thought about a great mass of foaming red hair. I thought about silver bands glistening in the sunlight. I thought about holding a figure that was so slim, and yet more exciting than if Venus de Milo suddenly turned to flesh while you had her in your arms. I thought what a damned fool I was. That didn't do any good. I bit my lip. I went to the can. I came back and had another beer. Even the beer didn't do any good.

Maybe I was in love. With a kid who thought I was lower than China when you try to dig down to it, harder than the look in Humph Bogart's eyes. And all for no good reason. But it wasn't just something for the animals. This was something with houses in the suburbs and babies and gardens in it. Gawd.

"Let's get on with it," I said. We had one more beer apiece, just to make the gallon, and went down to Riley.

"I'll steer Riley," I said. "You steer me. You know."

MacArnold directed us over to Westmount, along a block or two, and then up into the wilderness which is Westmount above The Boulevard. There the streets weave and wander among banks of verdure, behind which if you try you can see houses. Some of the streets may have names, but I doubt if anyone knows them. You are either born to this area of the continent or you find yourself a guide. I was born in Westmount, but below The Boulevard, which doesn't really count.

"Okay," MacArnold said.

It wasn't a big house, as hotels go. As houses go, it

was bigger than anything short of the Tuileries. It had been designed along modest lines with not more than twenty rooms, and not more than three wings had been added. It was stone, of course, and in the same architectural style as Windsor Castle except that it was bigger and had maybe two more turrets.

There wasn't a light in the place.

We circled in along a wide oval drive that cut over three acres of lawn and garden and paused under a *porte cochère*. We paused too. We went up steps and approached an oak door as wide as the Sun Life board table. I leaned on a bell.

"I better go back and move the car," MacArnold said suddenly. "Someone might want to get through."

"I left the keys in it."

"Oh."

No one came to the door.

"The servants are all down in the Servant's Hall, sizzled," I guessed.

I jammed the bell again. Then I beat on the door.

No one came.

"Early for them to be this drunk," I said.

"Try the knob."

I tried the knob. That got me nowhere.

I went back sadly to the Riley and got into the glove compartment, and got out the first-aid kit, and found the brandy flask. There hadn't been any other real emergencies lately and it was almost full. MacArnold helped me with it.

"Maybe there are other doors," I said.

"Sure," MacArnold agreed.

"Lead on."

The *porte cochère* door was the side door. MacArnold took the party around to the front door. We rang twice there, got no answer again, and finally tried the knob. The door opened. I won't say it creaked like the Inner Sanctum door, but somehow it managed to give me an eerie feeling. I began to get the vague idea something might be wrong. Houses like this in Westmount are not usually all dark at night. And if they are, the doors are locked.

"You've been here before," I told MacArnold, indicating the empty blackness before me. "Go in and switch the lights on."

"Yeah, sure," he said, "and have you heard about the Westmount police?"

"We are just looking for a phone."

"You look for a phone."

This was a place where the servants were supposed to be always in the house to keep the lights on and let you in, and as a result there was no switch anywhere near the front door. Nowhere my paws would reach, anyway.

I explored, with MacArnold at my heels. The corridor or entry was thickly carpeted, and our feet made less noise than our breathing. MacArnold's seemed to be getting a little thin and shallow. When I listened I decided mine was too.

I felt my way along the wall until I came to a door. This time the light switch was just inside. I turned it on. MacArnold jumped so hard against me he had to slide back down my left leg.

We were in the Senator's trophy room. There was a great bison head staring at us mournfully from over the fireplace, and a polar bear skin on the hearth that looked live enough to get up and claw. Over at one side of the room was one entire elk, mounted on a pedestal. The elk's head was thrown back and one hoof was lifted and pointed toward us. It looked sharp enough to go through the side of a Sherman tank. The elk looked startled. I'd hate to think how we looked to him.

The walls were covered with an assortment of weapons, none of your antique halberds and crossbows but mostly post World War One, practical killing implements. There were knives and shot-guns and rifles. There was even a Boys anti-tank gun, which you could only call a hunting weapon if you were looking for mastodon, and a Lewis gun which was strictly a souvenir of the World War Two home defense days.

But there was no telephone, and I chose that for comment.

"To hell with a telephone," MacArnold said. "There's nobody home. Let's get out. Turn off the light and see if we can't forget all that stuff is there."

"Who was left in this place after Kelloway expired?"

"His wife, and Carol."

"That's all?"

"No more family. There must be servants to run this pile."

"Maybe Carol and the Missus buried him, let the servants go away and caught the first cruise ship, to forget. Or celebrate."

"Sure, likely. Come one."

"Damned awkward," I said. "I wanted to talk to her."

I turned off the light and we headed back for the front door. MacArnold was ahead of me. Suddenly he stopped so fast I cannoned into him. I'm taller, and I hit my nose on the back of his skull and it started to bleed. I said a few polite words in Urdu, and when he didn't get those I cursed him a Lower Quebec French.

"Something's wrong," he said.

"Yes, there's blood on the carpet."

"I think I've just done one of the biggest double-takes in history. Something was wrong with that room."

"I'll bite."

He went back and turned the light on in the trophy room. We both looked around. Then MacArnold pointed.

I'd just seen it too. Beside the fireplace was a row of sheathed knives. One sheath had been pulled a bit away from the wall and was hanging at an odd angle.

And the sheath was empty.

I suppose it took us an hour to find that knife. We went over the ground floor completely first, switching on lights as we proceeded, finding nothing except a lot of rooms full of about $20,000 in antique furniture. We went upstairs and went through five bedrooms, each with its own bath, drawing blanks.

The knife was in the sixth bedroom.

I might have known from the size of the sheath. It wasn't really a knife. It was a machete, another souvenir of World War Two, the kind of knife they issued the Yank troops for jungle fighting against the Japs in the Pacific. It had a heavy handle and a blade about fourteen inches long and three inches wide. It would cut down a two-inch sapling at one stroke, if it was sharp. This one looked sharp. It also looked a little bit bloody. It was lying on the light rug in this sixth bedroom, and there was a stain under it on the rug. A dark stain.

I didn't have time to look for anything else in the room. I was beginning to be afraid, and I had things to do. I turned around right in the doorway and blocked MacArnold. "Don't come in," I said.

He hadn't seen the machete. "What's wrong?"

"Maybe we got trouble. Go downstairs to the phone and call the R.C.M.P. Tell them to get Dorset the hell up here."

"There's a phone in the study on this floor. At the end of the hall. I'll be there if you want me."

He went off and I went back into the bedroom. There

was nothing out of ordinary except the knife. The place was tidy and the bed was made. The door to the adjoining bathroom was open and no one was in there. The only place I couldn't see was the floor past the far side of the bed, and I went over to inspect that.

It was clean too.

MacArnold sobbed.

He was out of the room and down the hall and in another room, and it wasn't a loud sob. It was as though someone just beside my ear had sighed. Yet it carried all the way from where he was.

I got out of the room and ran down the corridor toward him, and he sobbed again. I heard one sob like it before. In France the boy beside me stood up in a shallow slit trench and was cut in two by machine-gun bullets. He sobbed once before he died.

MacArnold was coming toward me carrying Carol's body in his arms. At first I thought she had no head.

I guess someone had come at her from the front and cut her clean across the throad with the machete, and it had gone through just about everything except the vertebrae. As Mac carried her, her head hung down behind the body until the long blonde hair almost trailed on the floor. She was clothed in an emerald-green negligee and the blood, all that blood, looked black against it.

MacArnold's face looked like he had just been through Belsen.

I had a blockage in my throat that interfered with my swallowing and my breathing and my blood pounded until my eyes saw nothing but black. MacArnold was swaying in front of me with his burden. I thought it was me, but he was really swaying.

My stomach tightened up to something about the size and consistency of a baseball. Thank God it didn't decide to have sudden spasms. I had to do something.

Somehow, I persuaded him to lay her down gently there on the rug in the corridor. I got him under the armpits and shoved him into the nearest bathroom and sat him on the toilet seat.

He stayed there quietly. He sat stark upright with his knees apart and his hands hanging limply between them. He didn't move and he didn't say a word.

I went back to the hall. She looked almost alive, lying there on the floor, except for the blood. I tried to keep my eyes off her but I couldn't help looking. The negligee had fallen apart and she had nothing on under it. Her legs were long and tanned and very firm, with the smooth and not lumpy muscle that comes from constant and varied exercise at a dozen different sports. They widened to flat, perfectly-shaped hips and a taut, hard belly. The swell of her high breasts above that was covered partly by the stained-emerald green flimsy, but you could see they were all real. And above them was the ruined neck.

There was no expression at all on her face. Her mouth was calm and relaxed and her eyes were open and looking quietly up toward the ceiling. She looked just fine.

And if you picked her up, her head would fall off.

I couldn't stop looking at her. But inevitably, I began to feel sick. I began to suffer spasms that shook me right from the bottom of my guts. I almost ran toward the study where MacArnold had said the phone was.

He hadn't turned the light on in the room. The door was open and the hall light streamed in at an angle. It streamed on the body of another woman lying face down, feet to the door.

I saw her red hair, and from then on for about an hour I am completely blank.

Scene Fourteen

The room was a drawing room of the size that doesn't seem furnished unless there are at least four chesterfields in it. It had walls paneled in some bleached wood and wrought-iron chandeliers and pale-green wall-to-wall broadloom. It was damn near full of Mounties.

We were arranged in one of those cozy groups about the blazing fireplace, only it wasn't blazing and square in front of it, looking around at us, was the sagging form of Dorset. There was as much blood in his eye as there was upstairs on various spots on the floor.

MacArnold was sitting opposite me in a deep armchair, just sitting as he had on the toilet upstairs. He was in deep enough shock to need a doctor.

Ann was lying propped up on a chesterfield, caressing the back of her head tenderly and drinking black coffee. When I looked down at my hand, I saw I was drinking black coffee too.

"Then what?" Dorset asked. He was asking Ann.

"It was dark, and I'd sent the taxi away. I didn't want to leave. After I'd rung the bell twice without any answer, I tried the door. It was open, so I went in."

"Into a dark house?"

"Oh, the lights were on in the house. I meant it was dark outside."

"Yes, and then?"

"I called out, but no one answered. I thought perhaps Carol was upstairs taking a bath or a shower, so I went up. There were no lights on upstairs except in that study room. I went down there."

"And found Carol?" Dorset asked gently.

"I ... I just barely saw her. She was lying on the floor. I

couldn't imagine what had happened to her. Then something struck me on the back of the head."

"And you were knocked out until Mr. Teed found you."

I blinked. "So, I found her," I said.

"Yes. That was just before you phoned me," Dorset told me.

"So I phoned you."

I suppose I sounded a little stupid. Dorset asked sharply, "How do you think I got here?"

"Following your nose."

Dorset ignored me. "What time was all this, Miss Wedgewood?"

"I came here about nine o'clock, just after dark."

"And what time did you arrive, Mr. Teed?"

"God knows. What time is it now?"

"After eleven."

"At a guess, we were here at nine-thirty. But it took us anything up to an hour to find ..."

"Miss Kelloway."

"Yeah," I said hollowly, and burped, and was surprised and happy that it was only a burp.

"And this was just a social call you were paying on Miss Kelloway, was it, Miss Wedgewood?"

"That's right," Ann said. "We were friends as girls. I happened to be in the city today, up from New York on vacation, and thought I'd call on Carol. I telephoned and she asked me to come here. That's why I was so sure she was home."

If she was lying, and at least part of it was a lie, she was doing it better than I could.

"Did she say she was at home alone?" Dorset asked.

"No, she didn't."

"Why was she home alone?" I wanted to know.

"Mrs. Kelloway went away yesterday, to rest until the Senator's funeral, to the country home where she could be alone and quiet. She took some servants with her and let the others off on vacation."

"So Carol was deserted. How did you find that out?"

"I telephoned her at the country place," Dorset said, before he remembered he wasn't obliged to answer my questions. Then he got mad and said, "Please don't interfere until I get around to you again, Mr. Teed."

I stole a look at MacArnold. It was doubtful that he was fully conscious. He wasn't hearing anything or responding to anything. All this for the poor little blonde bitch upstairs. Well, she'd put my stomach off a bit, too. I wondered if Dorset would send one of the constables to find me a drink, but I persuaded myself to wait five minutes.

"Your occupation, in New York, Miss Wedgewood?" Dorset asked.

"I'm an assistant editor of a fashion magazine. *Chic*."

"I hope you were planning to stay in Montreal for a few days. I'm afraid I'll have to ask you to be available to us for further questioning. Have you relatives here?"

"I'm at a hotel," she said. "And I'll stay there."

"One of the constables will drive you there."

She got up, still holding the back of her head, and left the room with her escort, not even looking my way. I thought she might have thanked me for picking her up. Before I had time to brood about it, Dorset was at me.

"What were you and MacArnold doing up here?"

"We came to see Carol."

"Why?"

"For the same reason her killer came, I'll bet. She knew why the Senator went to New York."

"What's that Miss Wedgewood to you?"

He brought that one in right on first bounce, before I had figured what was coming. I stopped it with my chin. I'd played him to stop and consider for a minute after I told him I knew why Carol was killed.

I swallowed. "Nothing," I said.

"Then why were you holding her in your arms and begging her to wake up, when I came in?"

"I go for redheads."

"Redheads named Ann?" he suggested. "Ann. Remember?"

"Sure, her name's Ann," I said. "Didn't you know that?"

"What I'm interested in, Mr. Teed, is how you knew."

"You've got me," I said. "The shock of seeing Carol Kelloway like that was just a bit too much. I'm blank from about the time I found her, until a few minutes ago."

"What were you drinking?"

"Beer, brandy. Rye earlier."

"I see," he said dryly.

"Maybe she woke up earlier, before you came in, and told me who she was."

"Maybe. You're sure you never saw her before?"

MacArnold did the most useful thing I've ever known him to do. Just at that point, he fell out of his chair.

There were still about four Mounties scattered around the room. Dorset got them over and underneath MacArnold. "Take him up to a bedroom, and have that medical examiner fix him up," he said. They bore MacArnold away.

Dorset said, "All right, why was she killed?"

"Come out to the butler's pantry," I said mysteriously. He fell for it and followed me toward the back of the house. The Kelloways were wealthy enough to keep their liquor unlocked. I selected a bottle of Johnnie Walker Black Label and poured four fingers into a wide glass. The Inspector wouldn't have any.

"We better go over this thing from the beginning," I said, after two swallows to knock my tonsils back in shape.

"You talk," he agreed. "I'll listen."

"You'll talk, too, or we won't get anywhere. I know some things, but I don't know why the Senator went to New York. If you know that, tell me, and perhaps we can fit some of the pieces together."

"I don't know that. I may have a vague idea, but it's nothing I can tell you. Go on. Give me your part."

"Here it is. Brief. The Senator went to New York to dig up some information. He found it and wrote it down in his little black book. Somebody on the plane – obviously – killed him to keep him from talking. But they didn't have time to hunt for the notebook."

"But you did," Dorset said sourly.

"The killer knew the notebook held the information that would ruin him – the information he killed to keep dark. So he sicced three colored boys on me to get it back. They got it back. Then he found out Carol knew something. So tonight, Carol is snuffed out."

The Scotch was good. It was also all gone from my glass. I poured myself another one while Dorset watched disapprovingly. He still wouldn't have any, but he furtively licked his chops.

"I suppose you still think the Senator wasn't murdered?"

Dorset said, "It begins to look as though something is wrong, doesn't it? Yes, the medical report indicates he could have been murdered. Probably was."

"So I'm right."

"You may be right, but you haven't said anything. Some person on the plane murdered the Senator. The same person, or an associate, saw to it that you were robbed. And now the third item in the chain of events is Miss

Kelloway's murder. That's all you've said. That's plain and clear. You haven't told me who or why, because you don't know. Any more than I do."

"I don't know why, but I know who."

He didn't react. He didn't say anything. He would be happy to let me talk myself to death.

"The three colored boys who hijacked me were working for the Reverend Horatio White. White was associated with our blue-haired friend from the plane – Scarper. There's your man."

"White was on the plane too."

"He was too sick to slap a mosquito."

"That could have been acting." Dorset stopped and mused for a minute. His faded old blue eyes ranged the pantry idly and finally rested on the Scotch bottle. He cleared his throat but it couldn't have come clear, because he tried again. I guess it still didn't come clear. He got a glass and poured himself some Johnnie Walker.

He said, "All right, perhaps Scarper killed him. Or both of them. Perhaps White did. It doesn't make sense, it doesn't make a case, until we know why."

"I can give you the connection between White and Scarper," I said, playing my ace.

"I have it," he said, trumping.

"Why would Kelloway be interested in Scarper?"

"There might be a connection, in the metals field."

"So. Scarper was trying to play around with Kelloway's company's stock on the market?"

"I didn't say that. I don't know."

"Something else, then."

"What's Ann Wedgewood got to do with this?"

"Nothing," I said definitely. "Is everybody else on the plane clean?"

"As far as I can see so far."

"Well," I said, a little wearily, "I've got work to do. Want me any more?"

"No. You might see if you can take MacArnold home. By the way, how much have you told him?"

"Not enough to give him a story."

"Good. Stay where I can find you."

I went upstairs looking for MacArnold. He was face down on a huge double bed, crying.

"That won't help," I told him.

I took him by the shoulder and shook him gently. "That won't help."

He twitched my hand off. "Go away, for God's sake, go away."

"We'd better be getting home."

He stopped sobbing aloud, but his body still shook. Dorset appeared in the door with a remedy – the bottle of Scotch and a glass. He handed it to me silently.

I was bigger than MacArnold. I lifted him around and sat him on the edge of the bed. His face was sallow and dead-looking. It was stained with tears. He disgusted me a little bit, but I stopped and wondered how I would have behaved if Ann had been dead instead of stunned. Probably I'd have been worse. I fed Scotch past his unprotesting lips.

But it was no use. When I'd put a whole drink inside him and then waited for it to warm him up, he was still unhearing and unresponsive. I went out and found Dorset.

In the hall they had put Carol on a stretcher and were just getting ready to carry her away. They'd covered her, thank God.

"Are your men going to be here all night?" I asked.

"Yes."

"Let MacArnold stay there and work it off. I can't haul him along, the way he is now."

The Scotch was warm inside me. I staggered a little as

I went down the main stairway, but that was all right with me. I'd sooner stagger than feel things too keenly, at this point.

I got back to the Riley and he started, of course, like a charm. He found his way, with no gas at all, down a hundred winding avenues and crescents and places and things to The Boulevard. Along The Boulevard was home, and it had been a hard night. We steamed out to Cote des Neiges, across it and up a few yards to my apartment block. In the driveway, but then there was trouble.

The garage door was shut.

My garage door was never shut. It's a communal garage for the apartment block, it holds about twenty cars, and the door is perpetually rolled up. Now it was closed, and I didn't know quite what to do about it.

"Wait here," I told Riley, and idled him. I went over to the doors and pulled at them. They wouldn't budge.

I came back and sat down in Riley and thought.

A hooked arm came out of the darkness behind me, as suddenly as the steel bar on the trap when the mouse bites the cheese.

The arm landed against my windpipe and knocked out my breathing completely and gagged me. I tensed my muscles, and shoved, but I couldn't get away. And I couldn't get my breath. The Riley was a two-passenger, single-seater roadster. Someone was in the back, probably standing on the back bumper and lying on the trunk to reach me. He could reach me, but I couldn't reach him.

"Back up," a hoarse voice said.

I could use a little air. I slammed Riley into reverse and backed out of the driveway. The pressure on my throat eased a little and I could suck in wind. Nothing ever tasted better.

"Wait!" the voice cautioned.

Two cars went by on Cote des Neiges, quite close together, going fast. Then the street was empty.

"Back out," I was directed. "Turn down Cote des Neiges."

I did what I was told. There was still a little air left in my lungs. Then there was a jerk against my windpipe again, so hard I almost blacked out. "Go slow," the voice cautioned. "Go down Cote des Neiges. Slow."

I shoved Riley into high as we started to coast. I got what breath I could. Then I threw in the clutch and stepped on the accelerator.

"Slow!" the voice screamed, "slow!" The arm pulled back against my neck with mad force. I wondered how easily my neck was going to break. I had enough breath left for about another fifteen seconds.

We were coming down the steepest part of the hill, the place where you got straight down Cote des Neiges onto MacGregor, past the corner of Atwater. The Riley must have been doing about ninety. My vision was beginning to get a little black around the edges, but no vertebrae had cracked. That was where I put on the brakes.

I have never stepped on brakes harder.

I was braced against the bottom of the steering wheel and hardly even felt it. There was a jerk and my body and head came forward onto the wheel and flattened there. Over my head a dark form hurtled past the windscreen, the arm was torn away from my neck, and something was rolling on the road in front of the Riley.

Rileys don't stall. Even with that braking the engine was still turning over, and it pulled us on. There was a bump as the right front wheel went over the form, and a scraping, tearing noise as the oil pan caught in something and then pulled away again. The differential ploughed through something more solid, and then I was clear.

It seemed as though the whole thing had happened quicker than you could light a cigarette and blow out the match. I didn't quite believe it had happened at all.

I made a wide U-turn at the corner of Cote des Neiges and MacGregor and came back. Halfway up the steep hill I saw a large chunk of checkerboard-pattern cloth.

When I got up toward the body someone was standing beside it. I slowed. The man looked up square into my face.

He was a Negro. His name was Petey, and he had arranged a heist on me once before, in the Caravan bar. I shifted Riley down a notch to get all the acceleration I needed and took off up the hill. When I looked back, Petey had been joined by another figure and they were starting to drag the form off the road.

I figured it was one accident that wouldn't be reported.

I felt a little sorry for the smart, slim Negro in the checkerboard suit. But not very. I wondered if he was dead.

I began to notice my breathing. My breath was whining in gasps through my bruised windpipe, like a jet engine trying to warm up.

I hoped he was dead.

I got back to my apartment block. I left the Riley out in front, this time. To hell with the garage.

Scene Fifteen

I LOOKED AT MY WATCH as I hauled in my pocket for my keys, at the apartment door. It was after one o'clock.

I'd had a fine twenty-four hours.

I'd been slit across the leg, fed dope, slugged on the head, fallen in love and been choked. You can pick out your idea of which was the worst. I couldn't decide.

What had happened to me wasn't anything compared with what had happened to the Kelloway family. In the same twenty-four hours, it had been two-thirds wiped out.

Who by? For why?

I didn't even care. All I wanted was sleep.

I shut the door behind me. I walked over to the pretty little telephone table in the entry and pulled the phone cord out of its cute little wall plug so the darling telephone would be hushed until I felt like hearing it again. I turned out the entry light. That just left the light in the living room on. I didn't remember having any of the lights on, but I wasn't letting that worry me.

I went just inside the doorway of the living room and let my tired feet sink into the richness of my velvet-green rug. I put my hand on the light switch. I looked around at my light green walls and my dark green wall and my yellow-brick fireplace. I looked at the oils on the wall. One was a study of two sad, quiet nudes kneeling on a beach. They were oddly detached and calm and they weren't prurient at all; you could say that much for my taste. The other was a dim grey-green job showing rooftops and trees. It was a nice painting to look at just before you went to sleep. I looked at it quite a long time. I didn't look down at the chesterfield below it, because there was someone sitting on the chesterfield waiting for me. When I was through looking at the rooftops I flipped off the lights.

That which was sitting on my chesterfield yelled, "Hey! I wanted to talk to you."

"That wish is one I do not share," I said politely.

"Turn the lights back on."

I sighed. I couldn't very well avoid this. I turned on the lights and looked at a mass of marcelled blue hair that didn't match the black eyebrows and bloated purple face underneath it.

Mr. Ike Scarper. I sat down and looked at him pensively.

"It isn't logical," I said.

"What isn't logical?"

"That you should be sitting here waiting for me to come in, after you planted your boys downstairs to make sure I would not be coming in."

He tried to look shocked. He did it quite well.

"On the other hand," I went on, "maybe you didn't really expect me to come in at all. Maybe you were here looking around for something, because you expected I'd be detained. I like that one better. In a minute I'll check the safe and the liquor cabinets."

"I just plain don't understand, Teed. I think you'd better tell me what you mean." He was as full of stuffy dignity as a matron surprised in her bath.

"I'll make it very plain," I said.

I got up and started slowly toward him. I was pretty big and hard, and he looked as though he hadn't been in good condition since Mackenzie King's first term. It was going to be an awful shame, especially since the walls were too soundproof to help him much.

On the other hand he might have a gun. I almost hoped he did have a gun, a gun he would try to draw. That'd ease my conscience a bit.

I was about two steps away from him. I had my toes dug pretty firmly into the deep rug and my weight was well forward on them. I looked right into his narrow grey eyes and saw them flicker from my face to my hands to my feet and back to my face again. He didn't like what he saw in my eyes. His right hand came up like a flash and dived into his left armpit, and I left two deep dents from my toes in the rug as I jumped all over him.

He didn't have time to get the gun out of his shoulder holster. It went off with a dirty snarl, ploughing holes in my chesterfield. Then he dragged his hand out with the gun in it and smashed me across the shoulder. My right arm went numb but so did his hand, and he dropped the gun.

I didn't bruise my hands on him. I held him down with my weight and hit him with knees and elbows and the side of my wrist. He fought hard for an old man. He twisted around and got my hand between his teeth, but that only got his ear half torn off by my wristwatch strap when I dragged the hand away. He was licked and wouldn't admit it. He pulled his head back and gave me a face full of blue hair – hard. My nose crunched and gushed blood, and my front teeth loosened up a bit. Maybe I was unreasonable to get mad. I rabbit-punched him twice just back of the ear. On the second one he collapsed off the chesterfield onto the floor. On the way down he ran into my knee coming fast in the other direction, and air came out of him like a tire blowing out at seventy. He lay still on my rug. He was pretty blue before he began breathing again.

I looked at the chesterfield. Besides the bullet hole, there was considerable blood on it. Well, I was going to have it re-upholstered anyway. It was nice to know I could get Scarper to pay for it.

I dragged him up until he was sitting on the floor with his back against the chesterfield. I sat down on his feet. It wasn't comfortable but you have to make some sacrifices.

I slapped him with the back of my hand. I used the hand with the small diamond. It left a small hole in his face.

"Talk to me," I said pleasantly.

His eyes opened. For the first time, he looked scared.

All the venom and rage and frustration and fatigue that had been accumulating in my system for the last twenty-four hours welled out. I slapped him again. This time the ring left a jagged gash in his cheek. "You wanted to talk to me," I reminded him, and my voice wasn't nice. "Go on. Talk."

There was blood on his teeth when he drew back his lips. It didn't make me sorry for him. It was probably my blood. "What – do you want?" he managed.

"Why did Kelloway go to New York?"

"I don't know."

I slapped him once each way, once with each hand. The right hand didn't have a ring but it ploughed up some territory that hadn't been touched before. "I wanted you to talk," I said. "Lies don't count as talking. No lies, please."

"He followed me there," Scarper said. "He went down there to check on me."

"Why?"

"He thought I was trying to rig the market on him. He's been out to get me since I pulled a smart one on him once. But I was just there on a legitimate deal."

"Then why'd you kill him on the way back?"

"Who? Me?" he said like a cheap comedian.

That wouldn't get us anywhere. "Why were you in New York?" I asked.

"I can't tell you."

I hit him again. "Please. You're talking to me."

"I can't tell. Look, I could be smart and tell you a lie about it. But I can't tell you the real reason. It has nothing to do with you."

I sat there on his feet and waited for him to go on. He babbled some more from surprise at not getting hit.

"It's not my secret."

I waited.

"It's something you wouldn't even want to know. It's an affair that's been kept quiet for thirty years."

As they say in English literature, that gave me pause.

I looked at him for a long minute, figuring. Then I got off his feet and stood up. "Okay. You can go now," I said.

He didn't understand. He couldn't quite believe he was home free. I picked up his gun and slung it at the pit of his stomach. "Go on," I said. "Skip. Scat. Scram. Leave the premises. When I want you again I'll come find you."

"But I wanted to talk to you," he said.

"Fine. Some other time."

He didn't tempt fate any longer. He scrambled to his feet and the door slammed after him.

I allowed myself the luxury of a long stretch and yawn. Then I went into the kitchen and allowed myself the pleasure of a short pint of Dow. After that was gone I threw off the light, went back to the living room and doused the glow there and padded through the darkness to my bedroom.

The door was shut.

I never leave my bedroom door shut. Another night I wouldn't have thought anything of this, but I'd already had enough trouble from a shut door. The garage door had been shut when it shouldn't have been, and I hadn't thought fast enough, and now I had a little trouble breathing.

So I left my bedroom door shut and went back to the hall closet. I got out the shoulder holster with the automatic in it and buckled it on.

I went back and looked at my closed bedroom door but I just wasn't awake enough to cope with anything, not even if it was a stray breeze that had come through the window and slammed the door.

I put on the kitchen light and got a dozen empty beer quarts out of the closet under the sink. I brought them into the living room and spaced them in front of the three living room doors – not on the rug, but at its edge, on the floor where they'd wake even a Teed if someone kicked them. Then I went peacefully to sleep on the chesterfield.

I suppose I slept about two hours, because it wasn't even light when the crash came. It sounded as though at least six bottles had been kicked over and three of them had broken.

I must have been dreaming a B feature with hack dialogue because I sat up and said, "Don't move! I've got a gun."

There was a sharp intake of breath over by the bedroom door. That was all there was.

"I am getting up," I said carefully, "and going to the light switch. I'll have the gun trained on you all the time. Don't even let your teeth chatter."

I turned on the light. I looked.

I tried to breathe, but my heart kept socking my windpipe and knocking the air back out of my mouth, which was hanging open. I got that tingling of the spine that comes from a new experience, when you think there aren't any new experiences. I felt like a man who'd been adrift at sea for a month, had washed ashore on Bali, and was being helped out of his boat by the native girls.

I kept trying to breathe but it wasn't any use. I had to

turn the light off before I could pick up some oxygen.

"I'm sorry," she said in a small voice. "It was such a warm night."

"Don't mention it," I said hoarsely. "At least you left your pants on." Even if they are transparent, I thought, but I didn't say it. I was trying to act like a gentleman. The act had a chance of lasting another minute.

"Besides, I thought no one was home."

"I'm not a terribly curious man," I told her, "but I would like to know why you came. And how you got in. and why you went to bed in my bedroom."

"I wanted to see you," she said, "and the door was unlocked. And I didn't really mean to go to bed and to sleep. I waited for you in your living room a long time, and then I heard someone open your door. It wasn't you. I stole into the bedroom and closed the door and then ..."

"Uh-huh?"

"I ... I thought it would be fun to surprise you. But I fell asleep after I climbed into your bed."

Business was the last thing on my mind just then, but I wasn't anybody's pushover. "Why did you want to see me?" I asked her.

"Are you still trying to find out who killed the poor Senator?"

"Sure. So are the Mounties."

"I'd sooner tell you. I remembered something that might help. One of the passengers was carrying an umbrella. A hard, rolled-up umbrella with a curved handle."

"Ah," I said wisely, not giving a damn just then. "Who?"

"That colored minister."

"Ah," I said. There was silence.

"So you thought it would be fun to surprise me?"

"Uh-huh," she said. Forward, these Irish lasses.

"I could still be surprised."

"Well ... "

"Had a nice sleep? Feel refreshed?"

"Yes."

"You might go back to bed all the same."

There was no reply, but bare feet whispered on the floor. Then my bedroom door clicked.

I counted up to ten, just to give her time to reconsider. But even if she had changed her mind, I don't know what she could have done. There was an eight-storey drop from my window, and no lock on the bedroom door.

Scene Sixteen

I woke up in bright hot daylight, alone. Maida was gone. There was a suggestion of the fragrance of her hair on the pillow. That was all. I thought about her for a minute, but that was no way to start a working day. I got up and took a cold shower.

While I was taking the outer layer of skin off my back with an oversize Cannon, right in the middle of the second verse of "The Road to Mandalay," the doorbell rang. I draped myself and went out and let in Dorset.

"Just in time for breakfast. Beautiful morning," I chirped.

He looked at me sourly. Ever since he had started this case, he'd been as consistently sour as though they were keeping a quality control check on him. Open a bottle of lime juice, it's sour. Look at Dorset, he's sour. "Just about time for lunch, you mean," he said.

"So some people sleep in the mornings. Some other people sleep at night," I said smugly, "when everything is happening."

"If you are trying to tell me something, Mr. Teed, tell me right out. Don't be clever, please."

"You called on me. I insist. You tell me what's on your mind."

"Checking. I think I have your story. Do you happen to know anything of the whereabouts of any of the other passengers from that New York plane, last night, about the time Carol Kelloway was murdered?"

"You think the Senator's killer murdered Carol?"

"Answer my question, please."

"No, I didn't see any of them. I saw Scarper, considerably later. What's his box score?"

"He has an alibi for the time of Carol's murder. A good one. He went to a dinner party with some important citizens and didn't leave until nearly midnight."

"How close to the Kelloway home?"

"Fairly close. But I don't imagine he went out and killed her – and stunned Miss Wedgewood – while he was supposed to be away washing his hands."

"Stranger things have happened. You might look into the possibility. I still like him for the killer."

"I've been looking into him. I like him too."

"Unless you can pin it on the man who carried the murder weapon. The man with the umbrella."

"I'll bite," said Dorset stolidly.

"An umbrella could have done in the Senator. Horatio White was carrying one."

"No, he wasn't."

"I don't know how he ditched it before he was searched, but he had one."

"Who says so?"

"The stewardess, Maida Malone. She came here specially to tell me."

"And she looked like such a nice girl," Dorset mused.

"Go ahead. Insinuate. See where it'll get you."

"She's lying. The passengers were searched. The area between where the plane stopped and the terminal building was searched. The plane was guarded every minute from the time it landed until it and all its contents were gone over. There was no umbrella."

"I don't know where he ditched it," I insisted, "but he ditched it."

"I'll talk to Malone," Dorset said darkly.

"Shall we adjourn to the kitchen? I want my breakfast."

There was some pastrami in a back corner of the frig that was fine after I'd peeled off the green edges. Pastrami, which you may know as smoked meat, is even better with eggs than ham. I seared two slices on both sides and then broke an egg on top of each slice. That way they cooked without getting too greasy.

Dorset wouldn't eat anything but he had a cup of coffee with me. He was chewing something over in his mind. I thought he was considering my umbrella. I was wrong.

"Look," he said at last. "Will you tell me where you fit into this case? Or do I have to tell you?"

"I can't pass up an invitation like that."

"You will remember that you told me you were working on a case that involved the Senator. That is why you sat near him on the plane. You claimed the case had nothing to do with his death and refused to tell me about it."

"Right. And this particular case has even less to do with Kelloway's death than I thought then. Kelloway, as a matter of fact, isn't even involved in this case."

"That is correct."

"You don't know what you're talking about," I said rudely. "I mean, you don't know what I'm talking about."

"Oh, I do. You are employed by Miss Ann Wedgewood to find out who her father is."

I stared at him gloomily. Then I went over to the fridge and got out a small Labatt's ale. I poured it into a glass and toasted him before I drank. "I should know better than to pit myself, puny as I am, against the Royal Canadian Mounted Police," I said. "To the service!"

"Thank you."

"Merely professional curiosity, but how did you find out?"

"That bartender. The one in New York. Very sharp ears, he had."

"Nice work," I said.

"So you thought perhaps the Senator was Miss Wedgewood's father. But of course, he isn't."

"Of course," I agreed. "And up until ten hours ago, that would have been news to me. How, by the seven heads of the guardian dog of the gates of Hades, did you find that out?"

"Ann Wedgewood," he quoted from memory, "born 1922, March second. Carol Kelloway, born 1922, March third. Born ten months and three days after Senator and Mrs. Kelloway were married. Not too likely he fathered both, is it? Ever think of checking things like that?"

Now who was being smug?

"I found out. I found out he wasn't her father, my own way," I defended myself. "And I did better than you. I not only know who her father isn't. I know who he is."

"So you've earned your thousand dollars," Dorset purred. "Incidentally, I hope you've reported that money to the Foreign Exchange Control Board. Because I have."

"I hope inflation sets in after you retire on pension," I said nastily. "You want to know who her father is?"

"Certainly."

"Well I won't tell you."

"Childish, wasn't that? I'll find out. For a guess it was Scarper. He fits better than any of the others."

"He fits for the murderer too. I hope he is."

"We're back just where we started."

"That's not my fault."

Dorset got up to go. "I presume your interest in the case is now terminated," he said. He wasn't asking me. He was telling me.

"Nope."

"You are not in any way concerned with these murders, Mr. Teed. Not any longer."

"Oh yes I am."

"In what way?"

"MacArnold."

"From all I can gather, MacArnold had not been intimate with Miss Kelloway for some time before her death. I don't think that will serve as an excuse."

"All right, then I just want to see if I can work out the jigsaw puzzle," I said. "Or I just want to see a murderer hanged as soon as possible, if you like. A particularly nasty murderer. Did you look at Carol's neck?"

"Yes," he said unhappily.

"I've been dragged into this thing. The notebook is probably the clue to the affair, and I was the one who had it and let it get away. I'll work without a fee to get it back, if it hasn't been burned. Besides, a funny thing happened last night."

"What was that?"

"No soap. It wasn't funny enough to mean anything to you."

"Nevertheless, please don't hinder my work any more, Mr. Teed. Don't withhold any information that might be useful."

"All right. When I got home from the Kelloway place last night, they tried to hijack me again. The same three Negro boys. I shook them. I may have killed one, but I doubt if you find his body for quite a while. Afterward I came up here, and Scarper was waiting for me. He said he was waiting to talk to me. That's what doesn't make sense. If he told Horatio White to get the boys to salt me out, why was he here?"

"Four possibilities," Dorset said immediately.

"Okay. You set 'em up, I'll knock 'em down."

"He thought you would be safely detained, and came here to search for something in your apartment."

"I didn't have anything he would want."

"He perhaps thought you were getting ahead with the

case, had something that would incriminate him, had made notes."

"Perhaps. But as far as I could tell, the place hadn't been searched. And he was waiting quietly for me when I came in."

"He had searched the place without disturbing anything and was waiting to try to buy you off. He thought you had information on your person that he could either buy or take by force."

"Possible, because he had a gun. Unlikely, because he didn't try to use it. Until I made him," I said. I indicated the ruined chesterfield. "But we've beaten that one to death. Bring up number two."

"He waited to make sure his boys really fixed you. He would finish the job if they hadn't."

"Nope. He didn't attack me when I came in. I attacked him. In the interests of justice."

"So you say. Well, there. He had told Horatio White to have you spotted, but he didn't know it would happen last night. Meanwhile he had other business with you."

"That could be. But right now I'd like to work over number four. Horatio was working on his own. Has been working on his own all the time. Killed the Senator on the plane because the Senator was digging up the dirt about him. Sent his boys after me to recover the notebook because it had his record in black and white. Killed Carol, or had her killed, because she was the only other one who knew anything. Then had his boys try to get me again last night – maybe because something I did yesterday led him to believe I'd read the notebook, or otherwise was too close on his trail."

"You could work that into something," Dorset admitted.

"Leaving Scarper out entirely."

"Yes. Possible."

"Where is White? I thought you were going to talk to him. You haven't dropped any new gems about his character to indicate you've been in his presence."

"We haven't found him," Dorset said shortly. "We will."

"Maybe I will."

"I wish you would keep away from this whole thing. You don't know how much danger you may be in. My men and I are paid to protect people, but we can't stop a knife when a man sticks his neck under it. Remember Carol Kelloway."

"Remember Caen," I grunted. "I can look after myself."

Dorset looked me over. "You haven't done too well, the last day or two."

"You should see the other fellows," I said acidly.

Dorset grinned. "You're getting back into my literary range. Was that a quote from Tom Sawyer? Or Penrod and Sam?"

"Anyway," I snarled, "anything that can happen to me has happened. Go on, peddle your papers. Leave me this angle of the case for a little while. I won't stand under any loose bricks. You go find that umbrella."

Dorset shook his head, slowly and a bit sadly. "There wasn't any umbrella," he said.

Scene Seventeen

I KNOCKED OFF WORK that afternoon and devoted myself to MacArnold. He had got home to his apartment somehow, he had drunk himself silly on about three gallons of beer – he never kept anything stronger in the place – and he had the screaming meemies. Most of the time he thought he was with Carol again. Then he seemed to be going through a scene where someone came up and hacked off her head right in front of his eyes. It was not pretty to watch or listen to. I took as much as either of us could stand and then called Danny Moore. Danny came around with a big needle and filled him full of hippo oil. He put MacArnold so far under he actually went to sleep with a smile on his face.

"He'll come to with a hell of a hangover and no bad dreams," Danny promised, "in about twenty-four hours."

I told the landlady to drag him out if the place caught fire and left him. It was about all I could do.

Darkness had descended.

I had a medium case of the meemies myself, but strictly from hunger. I went to the Chicken Chalet in N.D.G. and had a large half-chicken. It was barbecued beautifully to a deep golden brown, the skin so tender-crisp and tasty it was almost the best part. The french-fries with it were small and well done, and the barbecue sauce was hotter than anything north of Dolores del Rio and approximately the best in the world. I liked it well enough to have another half chicken, and then I was still hungry so I tried to get a third. The waitress wouldn't take my order. She thought I was kidding her. I finally had to go to the kitchen and get the third half myself.

I sat and drank cups of black coffee and considered

what to do next. I liked Scarper for the murderer but it seemed to me Horatio was at least a strong contender. I'd better go see one or the other and try to get something.

If the Mounties couldn't find Horatio, chances were pretty good that I couldn't. I'd better go see Ike Scarper. I lugged a phone book to my booth and looked for Scarper. There was no Scarper in it. None at all. I could go back to my office and work over the city directory, but I was beginning to have another idea. It was vain of me, but I figured perhaps I could make women talk easier than men.

I got in Riley and whisked him up Decarie to Snowdon Junction. It was about nine o'clock, traffic was light, and when Decarie widened out past the Junction I could let him have his head a bit. He seemed to flatten himself closer to the road as he whistled along to the Sunset Strip.

Lucio's was one of a double line of spots that ranged either side of Decarie at this point, between the railway tracks and Ville St. Laurent. I saw spots – they were everything, from cheap drive-ins to fancy drive-ins to expensive restaurants to nightclubs of the country sort. Even to gambling dives – but that was in the old days. This was the Sunset Strip.

Most of them were the same basic architectural style – Recent American Roadhouse, long and low with peaked roofs and widespread wings. They were overlaid with trappings that disguised them into everything from Ann Hathaway cottages to villas from the Riviera to Burmese pagodas. And they varied just as much inside. You could spend anything from a dime to a century-note, depending on just which wide parking lot you rested your machine on.

I rested mine in front of Lucio's. It was a century note spot. There were other places a stone's-throw away where you could get about as much for a dime.

I got through the car-parker and door-opener, who

was dressed like a refugee from a Graustark operetta, only losing half-a-dollar and not paining him too much since I'd parked my own car. I encountered the head waiter before I could get anywhere inside. He was small and dark and as oily as if he bathed in baby oil.

"Good evening, Sir!" he said with the heartiness of a sideshow barker. "You wish dinner? I'm afraid all the tables are filled for the moment. Would you care to wait upstairs in the cocktail lounge? It wouldn't be long."

"I've et," I said simply.

"Oh."

"I just wanted to go upstairs to the cocktail lounge anyway." I tried to get past him.

"We ... we like to more or less reserve the space in the cocktail lounge for guests who are dining later. Perhaps you'd care to drink down here in the bar."

"Perhaps I wouldn't."

In the eloquent and immemorial gesture of headwaiters who have done all in their power to please an unreasonable customer they don't like anyhow, he shrugged.

"Look," I said, "I have a clean shirt on. I am wearing a tie and a jacket. I have money in my pocket, and if two hundred fifty dollars doesn't meet the bill I can sell you my car cheap. Can I go upstairs?"

He wasn't even looking at me. He was still standing in front of me, though. He gestured negligently with a menu the size of a twenty-four sheet billboard. "Why don't you go look in the bar. It's really very nice."

"I've seen it. It's just ducky. Now I want to go see Lorette Toledo."

He shrugged again.

I didn't have any more time to fool around, so I gave him ten rocks, which was about the standard fee in that place for just letting a customer do what he wanted to do. If I felt mean I'd take it away from him again on the way down.

The room upstairs they called the cocktail lounge was just a little darker than London on a night in 1941. It was quite a long, wide room and the ceiling wouldn't brush your hair for you unless you were as tall as I am. There were the usual chromium chairs with seats of plywood padded with plywood, or perhaps scrap iron, and shiny, hard-topped tables. The place was fairly well-filled with people who only had to accumulate a $20 bar bill before someone would come to tell them their table was ready in the dining room.

Over in one corner a baby spot splashed sickly-pale yellow light on a baby piano and a blonde with her teeth pointed out far enough to catch the light. She was singing a song about a man who was happy with two girls a night, but didn't quite know what to do with three. It wasn't a song I could really enjoy hearing, even if I was bringing along my dragon maiden aunt to discourage her from visiting me.

That was Lorette Toledo, what you could see of her behind the piano. What you could see was the blonde hair and the face and more of Lorette. There was probably a gown somewhere behind the piano, but it was held up about where an Englishman's belt holds his pants.

I looked around. In a very dark and inconspicuous corner, beside a door marked EXIT in red, a man was sitting alone at a table. He didn't have the tusks of a mastodon, but there the differences ended. He had all the hair and all the size, and he looked as if he had just as much meanness.

I pulled myself together and went and sat down beside him. He didn't notice me for a minute. He was too busy listening to Lorette and laughing at the right places, to show he'd read all those words on the lavatory wall when he was a little boy.

He glanced at me once, but he couldn't have recognized me because he didn't start to beat me up.

"Evening, Willcot," I said.

He peered at me. He saw who I was. "Goddam, you have your nerve," he said, surprised. And right away, of course, he got mad. "Get out of here," he growled in the tone lions reserve for keepers they hate. "Get out of here fast, before you get hurt."

"Before one of us gets hurt I have some explaining to do."

He was halfway out of his chair. "I hate scenes. I'm just going to break your arm quietly and drag you by it, out where I can work."

"You want to know who cleared you of the Senator's death?" I asked him quickly and quite loud. "Relax, will you?"

He crouched back into his chair, but his eyes kept burning me over like a pair of napalm throwers.

I said, "As soon as I examined the Senator's body, it seemed fairly obvious he'd been killed. That means everyone on the plane was a suspect. One person on the plane had done it. Maybe it was none of my business, but I wondered who. If I could help out the police by starting to investigate right away, it wouldn't do my reputation any harm.

"You were the only one on the plane who had any obvious link with the Senator," I told him. "I started with you. I had a little talk with you, without telling you the Senator was dead. You thought that was low. You thought I was pumping you. The hell I was. I was trying to save your horny skin, you ape. I was trying to see if you'd really

be surprised when you found out he was dead. Whether
you'd say anything suspicious before I told you. Well, I'm
not sure I'm glad, but you passed the test. I didn't think
you killed him. I still don't. And I told Dorset that and
told him why. I think he believed me. Otherwise, you'd
still be in a cell. Or you'd have Mounties hiding under
your table watching you."

I don't think he was much impressed by the recital,
but he didn't try anything else overt. He ignored me and
watched Lorette finish her last song. Then he stood up
and pulled out a chair for her, and she came out from
behind the piano and sat down with us.

Her dress was blue iridescent lamé, beginning at about
her tenth rib and swirling on down to the floor. The upper
part of the gown was clearly supported from the waist; it
was more like a bumper in front of her breasts than a covering over them. Some strapless gowns, a gentleman averts
his eyes when the lady bends toward him. This one, you
could drop a brandy snifter down inside and never touch
Lorette until you hit the belt.

"Good evening," I said, rising and trying not to notice
that her left breast was slightly smaller than the right.

"Good evening," she replied in the sexed-up voice.
Maybe she kept it hoarse by smoking hay.

She didn't recognize me. "I traveled from New York
to Montreal on your plane the other evening," I said. "I
believe we met at LaGuardia."

"Ah, yes." Vaguely.

"Actually, I'm a private investigator," I confessed. "I'm
looking into the death of Senator Kelloway, on my own,
and I wonder if you'd answer a few questions. If you
wouldn't object. And if Mr. Willcot wouldn't object."

I don't know what she had on him, but it was
something pretty good. She sat down and patted his hand.

"Mr. Willcot won't object if I don't. What could I tell you?"

"Briefly, let me sketch the scene. We are all waiting at LaGuardia for the plane departure. Mr. Willcot is sitting with the Senator. You are sitting beside a Mr. Scarper, talking to him. You get up, walk over to Willcot, say hello, and tell him something. You nod at Scarper as though it's something Scarper told you, and then you point to someone – the colored minister, I think – as though the message concerns him."

She frowned. Then she said, "Oh, yes, I remember."

"Would you mind telling me what was said?"

She laughed. "It was nothing."

"No matter how small it was, it might have something to do with the case. Because of the people involved."

Willcot guffawed. He sounded like a seal with a scratchy throat. "Oh, sure," he said. "I'll bet it did. Go on, Lorette. Tell him and get rid of him."

Lorette was tittering too. "Well, you see, Mr. Scarper saw me looking at Donald and asked me if I knew him. When I said yes, he bet me a drink I wouldn't go over and speak to him while he was with the Senator."

"So you did. Did Scarper tell you what to say?"

"Yes. It was silly."

"What was it? Please."

"He said I should tell Donald the colored man was very wealthy, and if Donald approached him perhaps he would help the Senator finance his new mine. It was silly, wasn't it? And it embarrassed Donald. But that's the kind of person I am. Always take a dare. And Donald's forgiven me, haven't you, darling?"

"I'm trying," Willcot grumped.

"Did the Senator hear this?" I asked.

"He was sitting right there," Lorette said.

"He didn't pay any attention, if he did," Willcot said definitely.

"Uh-huh. How about this Scarper. Nice man?"

"He was very amusing," Lorette said, looking sideways at Donald to see if he'd get jealous.

"A Montrealer?"

"I wouldn't know. I'd never met him before that evening."

"But didn't he say he came from Chicago?"

"Oh, he said something about being in Chicago years ago. I don't think he said where he lived now."

"You had a drink with him later."

She pouted. She looked shyly at Willcot.

"In the Caravan," I reminded her.

"I was just collecting the one he owed me. From the dare. Oh! I remember you, now. We saw you there. You were with some colored boys."

"I was with them all right. They weren't with me. Well, if you don't know where Scarper lives I'll have to try to find him myself. He's not in the phone book."

If Willcot hadn't been so sulky and unresponsive I never would have got it. But she needed more ammunition to fire at him. She reached down and brought up a small handbag. "Seemed to me," she mused, "he did tell me how to get in touch with him. In case I wanted him to buy me another drink."

Willcot looked at her with a pair of eyes you'd want dark glasses to face.

She pawed out a tiny address book. "Yes, here," she said. She gave me a Pointe Claire telephone number.

So he wasn't in the Montreal phone book. So he wasn't far away, either. I'd wasted a lot of time on some minutae and a scrap of information I could have found a lot more easily. Some nights you wonder how you can be so dumb and still remember your unemployment insurance number.

I smoke State Express solely because the package is light-colored and easy to write on. I got out the pack and put down the Pointe Claire number, thanked her, and left. I don't know whether she was sorry to see me go.

I know Willcot wasn't.

When I came down the stairs the headwaiter was standing ready to usher me into the dining room. Then he saw who it was and turned away.

I didn't figure I'd be wanting to come back to Lucio's for a long time.

I shoved him over to the side of the foyer and sat him down on one of the long benches that lined the wall. I sat down on top of him. I took his shoes off. I suppose I might have untied them first, but the laces broke before much skin came off his heels. There was a large hole in the toe of his left sock.

I took his shoes along with me. They weren't worth much more than ten dollars new, and they weren't worth anything to me. But it made me feel better.

Riley started with a throaty roar. He would have loved going out to the traffic circle and then along Cote de Liesse Road, where he could race, to Dorval and then toward Pointe Claire. I hated to deny him that. But I had something else I figured I'd better do before I went to see Scarper.

I buzzed Riley back downtown to Sherbrooke Street, parked in front of the Trafalgar and went into the bar. Jim got me a nice, light rum Singapore Sling and I took it into the phone booth, phoned the R.C.M.P. and got Dorset.

"Greetings," I said. "Still at work, I see."

"Yes, Mr. Teed." He sounded hurried and worried. "What do you want?"

"How's my umbrella?"

"No umbrella."

"Have you looked?"

"We looked before."

"Better look again. What I want is something different, though."

"Then please get around to it, and be brief."

"Where is Miss Wedgewood staying? After all, she's my client. You can tell me."

"Call me in the morning," Dorset said pleasantly.

"I'll tell you then. I'm not sure Miss Wedgewood is experienced enough to have the night lock on her door."

"Oh, come off it. You can always phone her and warn her I'm coming, if you're that worried."

"Call me in the morning," he said firmly.

"Look, I want to tell her who her father is. Right away because it'll take a lot of worries off her mind.

He didn't answer.

"Besides, I'll keep bothering you until you tell me. And I'll be a lot more trouble later in the evening when I'm drunker."

"She's at the Trafalgar," he said, and hung up.

That was convenient. I went back into the Trafalgar bar and had one more sling to celebrate the time I was saving, and then got her room number from the clerk. She was on the tenth floor.

"Come in," Ann called when I rapped on the door.

I came in. She was sitting on the edge of a turned-down bed in a black negligee that did things to her hair and skin. Things that haven't been done to hair and skin since Jean Harlow died.

All protective I said, "You should be more careful. It might have been anyone at the door."

"I knew it was you."

I sat down. A little deflated. "I'd be a sucker if I asked how you knew. A Mountie just phoned and warned you I was on my way."

"Right. I told him," she said a bit disdainfully, "that I could handle you all right."

"Thank you, Miss Aynsley," I said bitterly. It wasn't funny but it was loud. "Well, I came here to give you some information. But first you give me some. Why did you go to see Carol Kelloway?"

She shrugged, meaning it wasn't important, she didn't want to talk about it, and she wouldn't tell me.

"You went to school with her about the time Winston Churchill and I were at Harrow together, I expect."

"Oh, I'd never seen her before last night. The rest of the story was true. I called her up and asked if I could come to see her. I said I knew something about her father's death."

"But why did you want to see her?"

"I was going to see if she knew whether the Senator was my father," Ann said impatiently, "since you didn't seem able to find out."

"So you almost got yourself killed," I reminded her. "Keep out of this thing, will you. Restrain your detective impulses."

"I'll try. I'd hate to have anyone call me a detective."

"Who hit you?"

"I certainly don't know. I went into that study and saw Carol lying there. She was bloody. He must have been hiding behind the door when I came in. He hit me on the back of the head before I heard or saw anything."

"He?"

"He, she, whoever it was." She looked at me angrily. "Who was it? Margaret, I suppose."

"No. If I thought so I wouldn't tell you. But I don't think so."

"It's big of you to say that. You're really just saying it to make me feel better."

"Stop being snide. With your sensitive nature, the next time you employ a detective you better choose a retired clergyman. A real investigator says what he thinks."

"How would you know about a real investigator?" she cracked.

"Okay," I said tiredly. "Come on. Let's see how infantile we can get. But hurry up. This is the last chance. I'm going to tell you who your father is, and then go. And then the case is over, for you. You can go back to New York."

"Do you know who my father is, now?" she asked sharply.

"Yeah. I beat an admission out of him."

"Well. Well, who?"

"Ike Scarper. A middle-aged sharper with blue-rinsed grey hair, black eyebrows and a sizeable paunch."

"And he was blackmailing Margaret. He sounds delightful. He must have changed a lot since she knew him."

"I hope so. I suppose she has too."

Ann bridled. "Not essentially."

"Well, anyhow, I don't think she killed the Senator," I said. "Not that she couldn't have. I might admit that if I knew her, which I don't. But she didn't, because she had no reason to. He was not your father."

"I wonder who did kill him? And Carol? What a hideous person, to kill her like that!"

"Any murder is hideous. Scarper is hideous, too, in his cheap way. He probably did them in."

She blinked. "Is he that bad?"

"Or worse."

"I'll have to see him. I've got to stop him blackmailing Margaret."

I raised my voice. "You will not only not see him," I told her flatly, "You will stay the hell away from him. I'll stop the blackmail. That's included in your fee, no extra charge. I have to see him about other things and I'll fix that while I'm there."

"What other business have you with him?"

"I want to know who killed the Kelloways."

"Who's paying you to find that out?"

"No one. Revenge is my only motive. Whoever killed them has had me worked over twice. I'm striking back to maintain my frightful reputation."

"Frightful," she said rudely. "You said a mouthful."

"And twenty-three skidoo to you, too," I told her. I left. In the mood we were both in, there was no percentage in staying.

Scene Eighteen

RILEY WAS SITTING where I left him in front of the Trafalgar. The night was dark and warm and damp. You could see stars up through the spreading trees that weave over Sherbrooke Street, and it wasn't going to rain, but the humidity was high enough to make you sweat in reverse. It was a poor night for doing what I had to do. But it was a poor night for doing anything, and what I had to do would be unpleasant anytime, so there wasn't much to lose. I pulled the automatic out of my holster, let the street light shine blue on it and checked it. It was full. I took Riley out Sherbrooke to Montreal West, through Ville La Salle, and then along the Ottawa highway to Dorval.

I checked in at a roadside stand for a cup of black coffee and a look at a lakeshore phone book. I found Scarper, I.M., in the Pointe Claire listings. His address was the Lakeshore Drive, and the number placed him somewhere along the riverfront between Dorval and Pointe Claire. I turned Riley down the next street left, toward the water, and we cruised slowly along the drive looking for numbers.

Scarper's house, when we got to it, was a huge barn-shaped affair of white stucco, set back from the road in slightly shaggy grounds, and so close to the river bank it hung over the water. You could stand on his front verandah and spit over your left shoulder into the St. Lawrence. Even if you didn't have teeth.

Riley's lights had picked up the house number on the stone gatepost in front. The house itself was completely dark. It seemed to be the fashion in houses these days. I didn't like it. I didn't like it for two reasons. First, probably it meant Scarper wasn't home, and I wasn't likely to get anything from the house. Second, if he was there he was sitting in the dark laying for someone. Guess who? I give you one guess.

I left Riley between Scarper's gateposts, sort of on guard. I walked slowly toward the house and as I walked I took out the automatic and snapped off the safety. I started to put it back in the holster, but it struck me that would probably be wasted effort. I carried it in my hand.

When I came across the verandah to the front door the small moon was behind the roof of the house and I was completely in darkness. I had to grope before I could get the outline of the door and feel for the knob.

The door was locked. I didn't ring.

I eased along the verandah to the first window at the right of the front door. I tried the sash, and it was locked. I could have popped a pane with the handle of the automatic, but I hated to make noise. I put the gun between my teeth and got a strong purchase on the window frame with both hands. I pressed slowly upward. The house was old enough to be pretty rotten. The window catch tore away from the frame with a tired, creaking sound and the window came up.

If I was going to have to wait around for Scarper, at least I'd be able to wait inside. That was only fair. He had been waiting in my living room for me.

I went back to Riley then and moved him away from the front gate and into shadow behind some bushes. I came back to my window to go inside. And then I stopped. I wasn't waiting for anyone. Someone was waiting for me.

It wasn't my imagination, was it? It wasn't.

Something white was fluttering and flapping gently out of the window I'd opened. Something that hadn't been there before. Curtains.

When I opened the window the curtains hadn't blown out. The door of the room inside had been shut. Then someone had gone softly into that room to wait for me. But they'd forgotten to close the door after them and a draft from somewhere in the house, blowing toward the cooler air outside, had shoved the curtain into the night.

I was being laid for. It felt a little creepy.

Whoever was in there could blast me as I went to step in the window, where I'd be outlined against the light from the street. Or they could be waiting just beside the window to smash me neatly and quietly over the head as I ducked into the room.

No, thank you.

I backed off the verandah. I'll swear I didn't make any more noise than the fog drifting across the river under the moon.

Staying in the shadows, I padded over the grass to the back of the house. Here, at the river, the ground dropped away and the house was supported on concrete piles. Somewhere out on the river, behind the fog, a little boat hooted sadly like a lost owl. I jumped and hit the back of my head on a post. I saw bright lights for a minute. They were the only brightness anywhere around.

Farther down the bank where the piles were washed by the water I could make out the bleached greyness of old wood. A landing float had been built for boats just under the house. I went slowly and easily down there. Scarper had a big power cruiser tied to the float. It was a mahogany job with a low, neat wheelhouse. The bow was long enough to hide a motor the size of a diesel locomotive.

There was the slow rising and falling rushing sound of wind in the trees on the bank. There was the splat! splat! of little waves against the cruiser and the float. There was the dim, regular creak of the boat against her moorings.

There was a click, and then another click as a door behind me opened and closed.

Whatever had been laying for me in the front room had got suspicious because I hadn't come back. Now it was looking around the place.

I got behind one of the concrete piles and waited. For a long time nothing happened. Then there was a tiny creak as a foot stepped onto the float. Whoever it was, he was being very careful. I reversed the automatic so the butt was ready for use. Shots carry too far over water. I glared into the darkness at the place the creak had been. I'd need an oculist in the morning, I strained my eyes so hard trying to see something. I saw big chunks of blackness.

Two arms came out of that blackness, from right in front of my nose. They circled the concrete pile and me and closed behind my neck. Then they pulled, and they did a good job. They jammed my face against the concrete. It wasn't any rougher than a carborundum wheel, but you wouldn't want that against your face either. They jerked my arms against the pile and crushed my right hand and I dropped my gun.

I kicked, but all I hit was air and the concrete, and as I moved my face tore against the post like nylons on sandpaper. The hands holding me clasped tighter behind my neck and a thousand tiny pebbles bit deeper in my flesh. A man in a straitjacket might have been more helpless.

A quiet, polite voice said, "Good evening, Mr. Teed. You should wear a darker suit when you go huntin' in the moonlight."

It was a soft, slurred, warm, pleasant voice. It was Petey. "I'm very glad you came here," he said. "I've been wanting to see you since you hit Checkers. Poor Checkers, you broke his back. We had to shoot him, Mr. Teed, just like an old dog, to stop him suffering."

He had me. He had me – he thought.

His grip was high, around my neck and the top of my shoulders. I could pull my thighs back. I could pull them back far enough to get one knee up under my chest, and that was all I needed. The pressure of my knee was strong enough to lift my face back from the rough concrete and give me a little freedom. I put my other knee up against the post and heaved, and it broke his grip.

I was lucky. I might have rocketed back and into the river. All that would give me was a chance to swim away. But my back traveled a few feet and then slammed another concrete pile, when his hand clasp gave. I knocked the house about two inches west, but I got nothing except bruises.

Petey had fallen the other way on his back and I was on him before he could even move for a knife. We rolled at the edge of the float. I stayed on top. This was a kind of fighting we'd both learned in schoolyards and barrooms, and there is one thing about it: once a man's on top, if he's heavy enough, he stays there.

I was heavy enough.

Petey bucked a few times. The water was just below the level of the float and we were at its side. I stuck his head into the St. Lawrence long enough to weaken him up a bit.

When he came up, he yelled. I'm a little simple at times. I thought he was just scared of water. I thought that for about half a minute, until a door at the back of the house burst open and running steps smashed across the float and a steel-clad boot kicked me on the side of the face.

He missed breaking my jaw. He merely tore a hole through my cheek and splintered a tooth in my mouth. I shook my head to try to clear it. He hit me with a bank vault door just over my left eye. It had sharp edges. I went flat, smashing my scalp against Petey's mouth. He hit me again.

Scene Nineteen

CALLA LILIES, THOUSANDS and thousand of calla lilies were blooming by the riverside and the people were gathered at the bank to watch as the funeral barge came by. It was a great black barge and the black galley slaves who rowed it rowed with oars muffled by black crepe. I sat up in my ebony coffin with the black silk casket upholstery and watched the scene. I enjoyed it. Everything was perfect except the silence. There was no music. Maybe the orchestra barge that was supposed to come behind had been carried in another direction by the currents.

I felt a little cheated by the silence. I'd always wanted music at my funeral, and the Dead March from Saul. And there was something else wrong. Maybe it was the smell of the calla lilies. There was a heavy, sickly, almost foul odor in my nostrils.

It wasn't the calla lilies. It was me.

The embalmer had done a hell of a poor job on me.

I lay down in my coffin and went back to sleep, but I wasn't too happy about the way arrangements had been handled.

After a while I woke up again, slowly. They'd taken me off the funeral barge and laid me in state in some dim tomb, on a pile of rags. The smell was stronger. This time I didn't mistake it for flowers even on the first sniff. It was me. And time was passing. I smelled as though I'd been dead for quite a while.

It was a long time before I woke up again ... I guess. Anyway, everything was different. No funeral barge. No vault. I was in some kind of narrow closet with pipes for one wall. They were big, fat pipes and there was no solid wall beyond them; a bit of dim light filtered between them.

I began to doubt I was dead at all. The dead don't have headaches like mine even in hell.

But there was still the smell.

I got up off the pile of rags I was lying on, holding my head in both hands. The head got worse but the smell got better.

The pile of rags was the smell.

The pile of rags was the Reverend Horatio White. That is, it was the late Horatio White. Someone had worked on his head with the length of a lead pipe.

I wasn't really interested. I wasn't interested in anything but a cure for my head. I got to my feet and staggered the length of the narrow closet. It seemed to be full of pipes, pipes inside as well as along the walls, pipes of all sorts and sizes. At the end of the closet was a small square grating. I kicked it with my good leg and it fell outward. I stuck my head through.

I was back in the African Church of the Lost Lamb.

I crawled out from behind the organ, which was where the Reverend and I had been. I came down into the body of the church and found a door that gave onto a corridor. At the end of the corridor was a little office. Horatio's office. It was a small, square room paneled and furnished in that dirty, waxed light oak that is peculiar to cheap church furniture. There was a desk and chairs and on the floor a faded and worn flowered axminster that had formerly lived fifty years in some parishoner's home. Set in one corner was a tiny wash basin with no mirror. I went to the wash basin and began splashing water on my face, and wished I hadn't. The minute water touched me I stung as though someone had just fired a charge of rock salt in my face. I couldn't open my eyes. There was a metal clothes cabinet beside the wash basin and when I wrenched open the door I found a towel hanging inside. I wiped, gently.

When my eyes opened I was looking into the mirror on the inside of the cabinet door. My face, after the rub with concrete, looked as though a Chinese had got me well started toward the death of a thousand cuts. The whole left side of my face was black where the bastard had hit me over the eye, and the hole in my cheek where he kicked me was caked over and around with dried blood. I felt inside my mouth with my tongue. There were splinters instead of my last upper left molar.

There was a lump on my head, too. That I was going to have X-rayed. It should be a fracture. I must have stopped breathing for a while, or they wouldn't have thrown my body for dead, in with the organ pipes and Horatio. That was strictly their meat locker.

In the clothes cabinet was a black cassock tinged with iridescent green, two soiled white surplices, a big umbrella with an old-fashioned, straight bone handle; a tattered trenchcoat that probably saw service in the Boer War, and a pair of scuffed toe-rubbers. There was also a cheap and shabby black leather briefcase which had been upended, and the contents strewn on the cabinet floor. The contents were some typed copies of old sermons. I looked over at Horatio's desk. I hadn't looked at it closely before. The drawers had all been pulled out and their contents pawed over.

Someone had been looking for something.

I sat down in Horatio's chair and laughed. Oddly enough, it made my head feel better. I laughed for a long time.

I wondered if they had found it. I made a substantial bet with myself they hadn't. You could have said a lot of things about Horatio, but he wasn't dumb.

I wasn't dumb either, when I had a head. Today I had no head. I thought for a while, but I only had one idea. It was better than none at all.

I went back out to the organ and switched it on. Then I started along the keyboard, playing each key and listening for the note. It took a while. Finally I came to the foot pedals and played them one by one. I should have started with them. They controlled the big pipes.

The G-pedal sounded pretty sour. There was a sort of rattle to it.

I got two heavy hymn books and laid them on the pedal to keep it sounding so I could find the pipe. Then I went back in with Horatio, into the pipe rack. The low note was blasting right into the one dead ear they'd left him.

They were pretty dumb. They'd buried Horatio practically on top of what they were looking for.

I shoved my hand into the aperture in the pipe. There it was, stuck to the inside of the pipe with chunks of Scotch tape, just out of sight.

I pulled out Senator Kelloway's black notebook.

Scene Twenty

THERE WAS A BOTTLE of Berry's Best Scotch on the top shelf of my kitchen cabinet. I hated to use it that way, but I didn't have any other good disinfectant in the house.

I got it down and wet my palm with it and began to pat it on my face. It stung like the breath of a jet plane, it stung enough to make me forget how sore my head was. After the stinging subsided I felt a lot better.

I got down my biggest glass, the sixteen-ouncer, and loaded it with nearly a tray of ice cubes. Then I filled in all the space between the cubes with Berry's Best. It added up to more or less what I needed.

I came into my living room.

I asked Dorset, "Have they found Riley yet?"

"Sure," he grunted. He pried his eyes up from the Senator's black notebook. "It was reported early this morning, in about eight feet of water off a pier near Pine Beach. Man who lives near there thought he heard something funny last night and he looked this morning, and there it was. They drove it off the pier."

"Oi, gevalt!" I said, uttering the old Yiddish lament with appropriate sadness.

"Oh, the Riley's all right. They drove it back here under its own power. It's down in your garage now."

Good old Riley. Waterproof as an Oyster watch with the stem screwed in. "Was that why you started looking for me?"

"Why else? Your body wasn't in the car, so we thought we'd better try to drag it up. I called Miss Wedgewood first, but she hadn't seen you since last night."

"I know you were glad for her."

"I was," Dorset said primly. "Then we tried about five

of your favorite bars. When you weren't there, I almost gave up hope."

I lit a State Express to go with Berry's Best, and stuck it gingerly between my lacerated lips. "So how good are you?" I gloated. "So I get back here by taxi and tell you where I am before you find me."

Dorset looked at me moodily. "We'll find you yet," he said. "We find bodies quickly."

"I'll give you an explanation to that one, too. You didn't find Horatio. I did."

"True."

"I hope you've moved him. He smelt," I said, delicately avoiding the use of the work 'stank'.

"He did indeed."

"How long has he been dead?"

"Not as long as you might think. The weather's pretty warm. He was done in with a piece of pipe."

"It looked like something of that nature. Fingerprints?"

"No fingerprints."

"That scratches my pet theory," I said unhappily. "The death of Horatio, I mean. I thought he might have been the power behind it all."

"Oh, no. Certainly not."

"Well, dammit, I keep on saying I like Scarper. But I don't. And you don't. And we both know it. Why not? Because he's too obvious?"

"Perhaps," Dorset said cautiously.

"Look. Review. It is possible that the Senator, for some mad reason of his own, was after Horatio ..."

"We now know who he was after," Dorset pointed out. "We have his notebook."

"I'm telling you the way I was figuring before. I want to clear away the old line before we ring in a new one.

Let's say the Senator was after Horatio and Horatio knew it. So on the plane he slugs Kelloway with his umbrella ..."

"No umbrella," Dorset said. He almost yelled it.

"I have something to work into that angle," I said grimly. "Anyway, say he killed the Senator. He fingered me and had me brought in to get the notebook back. He killed Carol because she was in the know. But then, why did the boys try to put to snatch on me again after that? It doesn't add up."

"You're talking a theory that's been disproved."

"I know," I said, "but there's still that little matter of the boys jumping me down at the garage. You can't explain that. Anyway, that's what I wanted to bring out. But – okay, Horatio was a puppet in the thing. Kelloway was killed. The notebook was wanted, and Horatio was told to get his boys to get it. So they took it from me and gave it to Horatio. Then he made a mistake. He wanted to make a little money on the deal, so he hid the notebook. All it got him finally was a busted head."

"And someone else killed the Senator. Probably the same person killed Carol. And slugged Ann Wedgewood. And employed Horatio to get the book, and later killed him."

"It looks like it."

"Scarper."

"Who else?"

"It has to be someone who was on the plane."

"Yes." Dorset frowned. "That makes it beautifully simple. And again not simple at all. It had to be someone on the plane. At least, clearly, someone on the plane killed Senator Kelloway, and probably did all the rest of the work. But if it wasn't Scarper, who was it?"

"That," I said sagely, "is precisely the point that we're at. Which brings us to the notebook. What does the notebook say?"

"Titanium."

I took a deep slug of my Scotch. "I can see we've got to start away back. What's titanium?"

"A metal that's lighter than steel, yet stronger than aluminum, and resistant to extremely high temperatures. It's hard to produce from its ores, but processes are being developed. It's the exact answer to the problem of a satisfactory metal for building jet engines. And for a lot of other defense uses."

"Go on."

"There aren't many good deposits of ilmenite, or Titanium ore. One was discovered in Quebec a little while ago, in the Lake Allard region. Maybe you've heard."

"I don't read newspapers. Go on."

"The notebook says another deposit has been discovered. I'm telling you because you found the book, and you could have peeked if you'd wanted to. But keep it silent as a tomb."

"Sure, sure," I said impatiently.

"The new deposit is far bigger than the Allard Lake find. It's bigger than anything on this continent, and the ore is richer. The claims were made by a number of individual prospectors, but they are now controlled by three men. The three men were ..."

"Kelloway, Scarper, and – who?"

"Smythe. Anyway, Scarper set out to get sole control. The notebook doesn't say how he was working to get Smythe's share. But you know that."

"I know. Do you?"

"Clearly, he was trying to influence Margaret Smythe to have her husband sell out to him."

"Sure. By blackmail."

"He seems to be a specialist in that. He had the

Senator's number, too. Will you forget I told you this?"

"I will."

"Apparently Carol killed a man once. Hit and run, with her car, while she was drunk. It was hushed up. Scarper had all the details – according to the notation in Kelloway's book."

"Just how does the book read?" I wondered.

"It tells the whole thing, in a sort of diary form. I suppose he was going to burn or bury it later."

"So the Senator decided to go to New York to do what?"

"To play Scarper's game. Somehow he found out the deal Scarper had worked with Horatio and the Negro congregation. The extortion game. Kelloway went to New York as soon as he got this information. He counted on finding Horatio, preferably in his cups or in some even more embarrassing situation, and prying some proof out of him. Which is just what he did. The book says Horatio gave him a cheque, to Horatio, signed by Scarper, for five thousand dollars. Horatio hadn't cashed it yet. It's in Kelloway's office safe in New York. He was all set to pull some counter-blackmail on Scarper."

"So Scarper killed him."

"So you say."

"So what do you say?" I asked, exasperated.

He rubbed his hand across his slack jowls, rasping against his beard. "It doesn't seem like quite enough for a man like Scarper to kill for. He would have worked out a dicker with the Senator."

"Well ... maybe he killed on impulse, like I suggested just after the plane landed. It was a pretty perfect opportunity. Or maybe somebody did it for him."

I began to get a bit panicky. I finished my Scotch in a large gulp. "This is beginning to add up to something," I said. "Maybe somebody did it for him but he didn't ask them to. If you see what I mean."

"You mean someone who wanted to protect Scarper, someone who loved or feared him or who wanted control over him, killed the Senator. That points several ways. It could point back to Horatio again."

"Or," I said bluntly, "it could point to Margaret Smythe." I wanted to be the one to say it.

Dorset frowned. "Oh, I hardly think so. For the present let's go on assuming that Kelloway, Carol and probably Horatio White were murdered by the same person. Now, I can picture Margaret Smythe doing the job on the Senator. I can't go any farther than that with her."

"Nuts. Let's tidy up. What else is in the book?"

"Nothing. He'd just finished writing about Horatio's cheque, I imagine, when he was killed."

"Why did Scarper go to New York?"

"For a guess, Horatio wired him for help."

"Good enough. Now then, either Horatio or Scarper set the three Negroes on me to get the notebook back. And subsequently someone working in the Scarper interest, if not Scarper himself, killed Carol to keep her quiet. But then, why did the boys pick on me a second time?"

"Easy enough. Easy enough to provide a theory, anyhow. Horatio was killed about the same time as Carol. That didn't bring the notebook to light. My guess is that the boys were working for Scarper by this time, that they jumped to the conclusion you'd somehow got the book back, and so went after you. Petey might plan that without telling Scarper, which would account for his being in here when you got in."

"All right. It's a minor point," I said. "I think we have it all cleared up. Except for finding the murder weapon.

And the murderer."

"I guess so," Dorset said.

"Have you combed everyone who was on the plane?"

He grinned. "Everyone. Except Miss Florence Milsky. Somehow, I didn't figure she was worth it."

I went over the plane passengers mentally. "She was the ugly one," I decided.

"When she smiled," Dorset said drily, "she looked like a rake standing on end with teeth upward and pointing out."

"She was from the Bronx," I recalled. "She was in Montreal on vacation to visit a girl friend. Undoubtedly an illicit relationship."

Dorset snorted. "Even a Lesbian couldn't love that."

"I don't care how unpromising she is. I'm going to check on her. Why didn't you? Why do I have to do your work for you? What's her address?"

He laughed at me. He gave me Florence Milsky's Montreal address. "Go right ahead," he said.

"I suppose it won't get me anywhere."

"I suppose it won't."

I looked at him suspiciously. "You're holding out on me," I accused. "You know something I don't know."

"I hope so."

"Something about the case."

"One or two things, perhaps."

"Give. Come on, who got the notebook for you?"

He got up. "Go interview Milsky," he said. "Maybe she'll tell you." He departed.

I snarled at his back and then went to the kitchen and dropped three raw eggs into a big glass of beer. I had that for brunch and felt better. I went downstairs to inspect Riley. He was kind of soggy and about fifteen pounds of mud were deposited on and in various parts of him, but he was ready to go. We went out and cruised idly around for a while. We thought.

We added it up.

It was necessary to use an X to signify the guilty party, until a few more points were clear, but aside from that it was pretty straightforward.

X killed the Senator on the plane. Scarper approved of this, but knew about the notebook and realized he wasn't out of the woods. So Scarper told Horatio to get the notebook from me. Horatio had Petey & Co. bring me to him and took the notebook.

X then killed Carol.

Scarper didn't receive the notebook from Horatio. He got in touch with Petey directly and paid him to produce it. Petey then double-crossed Horatio. He and his lugs killed the Reverend, but they couldn't find the book. They went after me on the chance I had it. Meanwhile Scarper was trying to contact me to buy or scare me off, in case I knew anything.

That was it to date, all except for X.

The Riley had wondered over to Shuter Street and was ambling lazily down it, dodging the parked cars at the side of the road. And just over there was the Malone apartment. We stopped.

I realized at this instant that a man whose face was half white and half purple and full of holes all over wouldn't do himself any good calling on a girl. I stepped on the starter fast. But just at that moment Miss Malone – Miss Malone Senior – came out of the house and recognized me, but only because the relatively good side of my face was toward her.

"Why, Mr.—" she said pleasantly.

"Teed. Good afternoon," I said, bowing my head low and wishing I had a hat I could pull over my face.

She came closer. "Did you have a fight with a Mixmaster?"

she wanted to know.

Pleasant little old lady. "I was run over by a centipede with spurs," I explained.

"Did you want to see Maida?"

"Do you really think I better?"

"It's all right. She's not home. I'll tell her you called."

"Is she out on a trip?"

"Oh, no. She and the pilot and the co-pilot of the flight when the man was murdered have all been grounded. Just until the investigation is over, of course, so they'll be available to the police."

"Oh. I see."

"Wasn't that a terrible murder?"

"The Senator? Yes, it was," I said solemnly.

"I was thinking of the girl's murder. That was the work of a madman."

I looked at her very soberly. "I think you're right."

She put her hand on Riley's door. "My husband was a madman, Mr. Teed. He would have done a thing like that."

She was a funny little woman. I rather liked her looks. Fragile and beautiful. Like a piece of fine old china, if I may be trite.

But she had no need to talk to me like that.

"Are you trying to tell me something?" I asked her.

Her eyes widened. "Why – no, of course not. I'm just a talkative old woman. You'll think I'm bitter, to talk about him like that to a stranger. After all these years. But I'm not. I suppose I still love him, though I swore never to mention his name again after he left me."

"Love can be very persistent," I said, for something to say. I was uncomfortable listening to her.

"And madmen can be very lovable. He was mad for power, mad with greed."

There was a pause and I was expected to speak. "Was

that why you parted?"

"Oh, no. He found another woman."

I was talked out. "Ah," I said understandingly.

"But I mustn't keep you. I'll tell Maida you called."

She backed away from Riley and smiled, waiting for me to step on the starter and go so she could wave goodbye to me in her pleasant little way.

I was beginning to remember two or three things and wonder about another.

"Pardon," I said. "I know you don't mention his name, but I'd like to ask you one thing about him."

She looked angry, but didn't turn away.

"Was he a Montrealer?"

"Yes."

"Does he still live here?"

"Oh, no," she said. "He's dead."

Scene Twenty-One

I was on Shuter Street anyway, so I stopped off to see how MacArnold was doing. He was doing pretty well.

He had only wakened up a few hours before, and he looked fresh and rested. When I came into his apartment, he was even eating.

We exchanged a few insults just to set a normal tone to the conversation. I said, "I'm sorry I got you into that."

"It's all right. It's getting down to reasonable, night-mare proportions now."

"I could tell you something about her that would help you forget it."

"Thanks. I'll do my own forgetting. Let's not mention her again. Not at all."

"All right. I thought you might want to know how the case is going."

"Do you know who did the killing?"

"Yes. Not sure enough to tell anyone."

"Then skip the whole thing for now."

"Okay," I said. "I'll keep in touch."

I had to go a long distance to find Florence Milsky.

She was staying out at the far Western end of N.D.G., almost in Montreal West, below the tracks. The apartment building was new and shiny and expensive. The apartments were small and dark with little rooms, cardboard walls and few windows.

Milsky was even uglier than I remembered her. She looked like Jose Ferrer looks with his putty nose, when he's playing Cyrano de Bergerac. I explained who I was and she gushed all over me. The other girls who lived in the apartment, including the friend she was visiting, hadn't come home yet from work. So we had the whole place to ourselves to swim around in the gush.

"I'm sort of assisting Inspector Dorset, the R.C.M.P. officer, with this case," I told her. "He asked me if I'd drop out and interview you."

"Anything I can do," she mouthed. "Anything at all." She was very hearty with this offer of assistance, and sprayed me with drips blown off her fangs.

I backed away and sat down in a small straight chair with no others near it. "Perhaps you remember something of what went on during the flight?"

"Not very much, I'm afraid. "You see –" she blanched, "thinking of it – I was so sick."

"Oh. I'm sorry."

"I was – you know, sick. Then I was so miserable and exhausted I just made my seat into a double and curled up with a blanket. I didn't wake up until we were coming down at Dorval."

"I see."

"I wish I could help you more."

"You didn't know any of the other passengers on the plane?"

"I'd never seen any of them before."

"Well, thank you," I said.

Complete blank. I left her.

I went down three flights of stairs to the street. It hit me. I went back up the three flights and knocked on her door.

"Why, Mr. Teed!" she said when she opened it. Just as if I'd been gone a week. "How nice! Come in."

I know danger when I see it. I stayed at the door. "You were saying you made your seat into a double."

"Why, yes. You know."

"No, I don't know," I said patiently.

"I pulled out the arm in the center of the double seat.

The one that divided it into two. That leaves one big double seat you can curl up in."

"Is it easy to do?" I asked her.

"You haven't done much plane travelling, have you?"

"Millions of miles," I said, "but I'm just not observant."

"All you do is lift a little catch down at the bottom of the arm. Then it pulls right out."

"Ah," I said absently. "Well. Thank you again."

I took Riley to the nearest drugstore and got on the phone. Dorset was in his office.

"You old bastard," I said. To let him know I wasn't kidding I went on back through about four earlier generations of his family, describing them as graphically as I could. It didn't make him mad. He laughed at me.

"Florence give you a rough time?" he asked.

"You knew all the time!" I yelled at him. "You knew all along, and you wouldn't tell me. That's why you were so sure there wasn't any umbrella."

"Oh. How the Senator was killed. Yes, we knew after the postmortem. The shape of the wound, after a closer look, gave us a good idea what to look for."

"I suppose you even know whose chair arm did it."

"I know which chair arm did it," he admitted. "It doesn't tell us anything definite."

"Which was it?"

"No soap," he said. "You might jump to conclusions."

"No fear. I've got my conclusions. You better work fast if you want to clean this thing up yourself. Because I'm going to bust it wide open all over the city in less than a few hours."

"Go ahead," he said. "Don't get yourself murdered, that's all. I might feel partly responsible. My hands are tied. I know who I want to arrest but I can't get evidence."

"I'll get evidence."

"Don't provide it by becoming a corpse. I'm not quite that anxious to finish off the case quickly."

"Nuts," I said and hung up. I spent another nickel and called MacArnold.

"Story," I said.

"You keep in touch very nicely," he told me.

"Not yet the story. But hold yourself ready. It's going to be pretty good."

"Fine. I'm drinking coffee trying to soak up the last of this laudanum I was jabbed with. I'll stay here and drink more coffee."

I hung up and ran back to Riley.

Maybe Scarper hadn't done this. To be definite, of course he hadn't. But just as definitely, he knew who had.

I figured to go see him and pry it out of him.

I make an awful lot of mistakes.

Scene Twenty-Two

IT WAS UNCOMFORTABLE down there in the bilge.

They hadn't pumped the boat out for a while and the bilge water was pretty deep. It was deep enough to wash in and out of one or the other of my ears unless I looked straight up at the dark night sky above. And I was getting awfully tired of squinting at the top left star in Ursa Major.

There was a wad of cloth the size of a winter sock stuffed in my mouth and held with adhesive tape. There was fifty feet of good manila rope around my wrists, body and ankles. It had been tied tight to start, and down there in the water it was shrinking fast as unsanforized cotton.

There were two fifty-foot lead weights tied to my feet. I don't know where they got them. Probably they kept them around for occasions like this.

It had all been very simple. No muss, no bloodshed.

I'd parked Riley a distance down the road from Scarper's, walked to his front door and rung. Bing, the big black gorilla of a razor-slicing Negro, answered. I backed him up against the wall and put a shot an inch from his ear to encourage him to tell me where Scarper was. Scarper was in the front room. I went in with Bing in front of me, but he didn't even draw a gun. That made two of them against the wall. I was standing where I could cover the door.

So Petey walked along the verandah, stuck his head and his gun in the window and heisted me. All very simple.

Simple Teed, I'm called. And with reason.

So here I was.

I'd been lying in the bottom of the boat for some hours. I guess they were waiting for it to get dark and quiet. Then it seemed just barely possible they might be planning to take me for a short boat ride and dump me in the river. The big mahogany cruiser was anchored there at the float under the Scarper house, as it had been the night I tangled with Petey. It was a lovely boat. I was looking forward to my ride in it. But I wished it was going to be a longer ride.

Every once in a while I got energetic and tried pulling against the ropes, but that just chafed skin off my wrists and ankles. Or I tried rubbing the adhesive tape of my face against my shoulder, but that just got me a snootful of bilge.

Eventually they came down to the boat: the three, Bing, Petey and Scarper. Petey looked me over and checked the ropes to make sure they were still tight.

Scarper started the engine, Bing cast off and we started out from shore. They traveled without running lights. A few yards out into the river and we sliced into a bank of fog and stayed there. You couldn't see the stars any longer. It was blacker and thicker than the bottom of a barrel of diesel oil. Scarper throttled down his smooth motor and we ran along in almost complete silence. Even after my eyes got used to the dark I couldn't see any of the three of them and I doubt if they could see each other.

Petey said in his quiet, soft voice, "I'm glad we're getting rid of him this way. He was too hard a skull for my liking. I would swear he was dead when we left him in the church."

Scarper grunted. His oily tones came from the direction of the wheel. "Leaving anyone in the church was a silly idea. Look what happened. They must have found White by now, since this one got out."

"I was going to burn the church down tonight," Petey said calmly. "It was too light when I brought him there this morning. But I was going to burn it down tonight and get rid of the bodies and the notebook too. I still think Horatio hid it somewhere in there. It certainly wasn't in his rooms."

"That book has got to be found and destroyed," Scarper said. "It's almost worth my life to have it still around."

"I'll find it," Petey said softly.

"You'd better. You've botched things nicely, so far. What's wrong with you? I thought you were clever. First you go after this clod for no really good reason, put him on his guard and get one of your boys killed. I could have told you he didn't have the book. Then you kill Horatio – without making him tell where the book is. You leave his body where it will be found and you leave Teed before he's even a body."

Petey chuckled. "I put Teed on his guard, did I? It hasn't helped him very much."

"The big thing is the notebook. If it says what it probably does and if anyone finds it except us, I'm through."

I snickered. Too bad the gag was too tight for them to hear me.

There was no more talk for a while. There was a rustle of clothing and the soft pad of quiet shoes on the deck planks, as though they were shifting positions, I don't know what they were doing. I couldn't see anything.

There was a sudden sharp intake of breath from someone and a slight thud practically instantaneous with it. "Damn!" grunted Scarper. His voice came from the bow of the boat now. "Stubbed my toe," he complained.

"You left the wheel," Petey said irritably from the stern.

"It's all right. I tied it back. Just wanted to see if I could glimpse anything ahead through this fog."

"Bing! Where's Bing?"

"Right here," Scarper told him. I heard footsteps returning.

I saw a shadow a little deeper than the rest of the darkness, directly over me. It was Scarper and it spoke. "Maybe we should take his gag off and talk to him. Maybe he knows something about the book."

"He'll only lie," Petey warned. "Or stall."

"Can't do any harm. He won't yell, not more than once." He reached down and got his fingernails under the edge of the adhesive tape. He ripped it off, not taking more than two square inches of skin with it.

I worked with my lips and teeth and got the cloth wad pushed out. My mouth felt as though I'd been eating winter underwear for a week. It took a long time for any moisture to drain into it, but I wasn't going to dampen it with bilge. The boat ploughed silently on through the black.

"I won't yell even once," I said finally. "I don't have to."

This struck Petey as humorous and he laughed, mildly.

"I don't think you'll throw me over. It wouldn't do any good."

"It won't do any harm," Scarper pointed out. "And somehow it's just one of those things I want to do."

"It would be your first murder count," I pointed out. "You haven't killed anyone yet. You were really responsible for the deaths of Kelloway and Carol and Horatio, but you didn't kill them. When they catch you, you might get clear with a smart lawyer. If you bring me back."

"No one's going to get caught," Scarper said easily.

"You want to know where the notebook is? The Mounties have it."

Petey laughed. "You see? I told you he'd start trying to pull a stall."

"Okay, Dumbo, I'll tell you in detail," I said. I described where the book had been, how I'd found it and what I'd done with it.

Scarper laughed. A very bitter laugh. "The old fat boy was too cute for you," he told Petey.

Petey corrected him. "Too cute for us."

"What are you going to do with me?" I insisted. "We haven't settled that yet. You're through now, all of you. Are you going to make it worse by dumping me?"

"I don't think that would make it any worse," Petey argued.

"Listen to him," I said peevishly to Scarper. "He talks great sense. He's been right so often before."

"This time I'm inclined to agree with him," Scarper told me.

"Yeah? You're all fairly close to being in the clear, right until the time you dump me off the boat. You didn't murder Kelloway and Carol, Scarper. Neither did Petey. And if Petey and his boys did give Horatio the lead pipe treatment, no one's worrying too much about that. He wasn't any great loss, and I doubt if anything could be proved anyway. But kill me? Why, it would be almost as bad as killing a cop. I've been working with the R.C.M.P. on this case for the past few days. I'm even beginning to be friendly with them."

"Up to a point, you're right," Scarper said. "But nobody is likely to get anyone for killing you. You'll just drop quickly to the bottom of the lake and stay there. They'll never even find your body."

"Inspector Dorset knows where I am," I said smugly. "He'll know where to start looking."

A light went on.

Lying in the bottom of the boat I could only see a dim glow to my left, above the side of the boat, but it must have been a pretty bright light. Petey and Scarper both rushed to that side of the boat. Petey stepped on my stomach on the way.

"I didn't know we were that close to shore," Petey said nervously.

"The wheel is set to take us in a wide circle," Scarper explained. "We're back near my place just now, heading out again."

"The light went on at your place!"

"I'm afraid you're right."

"Hell! Someone must have been following Teed."

"We can't do anything about that now."

"We better get out of here fast."

"We're heading out from shore again now. I'm not going to take the chance of revving the motor up."

"We should have gone straight out and dumped him," Petey grumbled.

"As long as he keeps on talking, he may say something."

"I have a good mind to bust up this whole party right now," I threatened.

"Ha, ha, ha," Petey said.

"There. The light's gone out," Scarper called from the side, relief in his voice.

"Petey," I said, "I told you once before you were working for the wrong man. You've changed bosses since then, but you haven't bettered yourself."

This time, Scarper laughed at me.

"This snake," I said, "would double-cross you faster than a bum picks a long butt off the sidewalk. Sooner or later you'll know too much about him, and then you're through. I think you know too much now."

"Yeah?" Petey was scornful.

"Yeah. So he stubbed his toe at the bow of the boat, did he? Where's Bing? See if you can find Bing."

"Bing's right there," Petey said. "Bing!" he called softly. There was no answer. He called again, louder. "Guess he went to sleep," he said easily to Scarper. "He's always doing that. I'll go wake him up."

"Oh, why bother?" Scarper said. "While he's asleep he can't make any noise."

"I'll just see," Petey said. He padded to the front of the boat. I was praying he'd find what I expected. I guessed he would because I heard Scarper moving quietly behind me, getting ready for trouble.

Petey came back. "Bing's dead," he said. There was an animal fear and rage in his voice. "What do you think you're pulling, you bastard?"

Scarper's voice cracked like a whip. "Sit down there quietly," he said. "I've got a gun."

Petey laughed at him. "I've got a knife. I like that better." He began moving slowly toward Scarper.

"I like knives because they always work," he said. "Not like guns. Guns don't work unless they have shells. Did you check your gun lately, Mr. Scarper?"

He was past me now, moving toward the stern of the boat and Scarper. He spoke again. "Maybe I didn't quite trust you, Mr. Scarper. Or maybe I just thought you'd get nervous and make noise with your gun somewhere we had to keep quiet. You'll never know which. Sleep tight, Mr. Scarper."

Scarper must have jumped him just before he got to the stern. There was a lot of grunting and heavy breathing behind and above me. They were standing, wrestling back and forth at the side of the boat. Then there was a long, gurgling sob. That would be Petey's knife in Scarper's lung.

Scarper had enough breath left for one more effort, apparently; or else he just collapsed, dragging Petey with him. They went over the side with a heavy, stinging splash.

The water collected itself together smoothly over their heads and there was silence except for the dim throb of the motor, carrying the boat on its endless circle.

Petey broke water. He screamed, and the scream ended in a gurgle. After a minute his voice came again, fainter and from quite a distance astern. "I can't swim!" he screamed.

"Not much I can do about it," I called to him pleasantly. But I don't expect he heard me. I expect he was gone for good by the time I spoke.

It couldn't have ended more prettily.

Except it wasn't quite ended yet and here I was circling around in a boat until it ran out of gas, or until morning came and someone put out to get me.

We ran on. I didn't have any idea where we were. Maybe we had circled back near shore again. "'Hoy!" I yelled. "Halp!"

In the distance I heard the sound of oars.

"This way! Halp!" I yodeled again.

Someone called, "I can't see you! Keep yelling till I get close to you."

I sang "The Road to Mandalay" at the top of my lungs.

Not much later, the sound of rowing approached from left front. Another boat grated against the hull. Someone clambered up, tied his boat, and put a flashlight on me.

"I thought you were going to keep in touch," MacArnold said.

"Loosen this rope and I'll keep in touch," I yapped at him. "I'll touch you in a dozen places. How did you get here?"

"When you didn't report back I called Dorset and was very nice to him. He said he thought you'd gone out here. What's the score?"

"Oh, very good for one evening. Three more corpses. Will you for the love of Jezebel untie me?"

He worked on the ropes. "Who got bumped?"

"Scarper, I'm happy to say. And two of the colored boys who jumped me the night at the Caravan."

"Where's the third?"

"He and I were involved in a fatal accident yesterday. Fatal to him."

"So the whole thing is cleaned up," MacArnold said. He didn't try to sound displeased.

"Not by a long shot. Scarper didn't kill the Senator. He didn't kill Carol, either."

"Who the hell did?"

"I can't tell you just yet. Oh, why the devil don't you leave that light on at Scarper's so we could see to get back there?" I headed back for the wheel and untied it.

"I know about where it is from here," MacArnold said, "I'll steer. It's not far. How did these three lugs get bumped? You weren't in a position to do them much damage."

"Scarper was double-crossing the boys," I said. "They knew too much about him. If they died nobody could prove anything much. The Senator had written what he knew about Scarper in a little notebook, but that was before anyone got killed and the only material in there was scandal and an extortion rap that would likely slip off Scarper. So he was clear when the boys were rubbed, and me, and perhaps later on the real murderer. He used this trip for sinking me as a good time to sink them too. But I spilled the beans after he got one of them. The second knifed him and then fell overboard and drowned."

"That's nice," MacArnold said.

We came to Scarper's float. "Call Dorset and give him the news," I said. "I have to go see someone." I lit out for Riley.

Scene Twenty-Three

I RAN ALL THE WAY to Riley. I turned him around and took off down the Lakeshore Road toward Montreal. We went so fast along the road that Riley almost lost his right headlight on one of the stone gateposts of the Royal St. Lawrence Yacht Club, pulling out of a curve in Dorval. We took the six miles of Cote de Liessè Road between Dorval and Decarie Boulevard in four minutes flat, and then we came down Decarie toward Sherbrooke only slowing to forty for red lights.

The evening was not yet over.

Live murderers keep murdering. Mine wasn't dead yet.

I cruised east on Sherbrooke, ignoring everything except police sirens and moving vans, and slid to a stop in front of the Trafalgar.

I was scared. Not for myself, but I was scared.

I got to Ann's room. I tried the knob without knocking first. The knob turned under my hand and the door opened.

Dorset had been bending over an open suitcase that sat on a stand at the foot of the bed. He jerked upright, surprised, and stared at me.

"Where's Ann?" I panted.

"I thought I left that door locked," Dorset said mildly.

"*Where's Ann?*"

"She went out about fifteen minutes ago."

"Alone?"

"Alone, in a taxi."

"Hah," I said glumly. "Alone. That's something."

"And why are you here?"

"Just about everybody's been killed. Except the murderer – and Ann, and her mother. I don't want to see any more killings." I told him all about what had happened out on the Lakeshore.

"That disposes of the murderer," he said.

"No it doesn't. What do you mean?"

"Maybe I should say it disposes of one murderer. We found Petey's fingerprints on that piece of pipe in the church – the pipe used to murder Horatio."

"Fine," I said. "All we have to do now is find the principal murderer. The one who did the two important ones."

"We have a wide field. A million Montrealers."

"Come off it. We have a field of a dozen or so. The people who were on the airplane, or at least those who are now left. One of them committed both."

"I suppose so."

"As far as can be seen, the Senator's murder was done for one of two reasons. Either someone hated him, or someone was trying to help out Scarper."

"Of those two, which would you choose?" Dorset asked.

"I was on the wrong track for a while. You see, I thought the Senator was Ann's father. Ann's father was trying to blackmail Margaret. So Margaret slugged Ann's father, e.g., the Senator. That's the 'hatred of the Senator' motive."

"But there were two things wrong with that," Dorset commented. "First, Scarper rather than Kelloway had fathered Ann. Second, the killing of Carol. If the Senator had been killed out of hatred, the killer had nothing to fear from Carol. But if he had been killed because of the purpose of his New York trip – because he was investigating Scarper – Carol knew something that would make her suspicious. So she had to be silenced. Yes, the motive of the murder was to put Scarper in the clear. The motive for both murders."

"Right. Well, who was connected with Scarper? First of all, Horatio. He was too sick to kill and didn't have the guts to do it anyway. Then there was Lorette Toledo. She turned out to have just a casual connection with Scarper. That washes out Donald Willcot too, because his only connection with Scarper was through Lorette. I've thought of both of them but I think we can cross them off the list."

"Who does that leave who was connected with Scarper?"

"I think you know," I said, "so I won't tell you. It isn't all clear yet, anyway."

"It's far from clear. For instance, you haven't told me yet why you know Scarper himself didn't do the killing."

"Mostly a feeling," I admitted. "A feeling that someone else was responsible."

"Feelings aren't reliable things to go on in a murder investigation."

"All right. First, he was the type who didn't do his own killing. Second, like the others, he was too sick to pull off a slick and risky killing like the one on the plane. Third, he was in a bad position to do it. Garnett and LaRouche, the press man and the salesman, were between him and the Senator. So was Don Willcot and so was I. But the clincher was the murder weapon. When I knew what that was I was sure he didn't do it. You see, there were no empty double seats between Scarper and the Senator. It would be too risky for Scarper to go to the front or back of the plane, get a chair arm, kill with it and then walk around again to put it back. That only left his own chair arm to use. And Lorette Toledo was sitting with him."

"He couldn't have taken the arm without her knowing?"

"Nuts. I don't care how sick she was – she would have

noticed. And she would have let it drop sometime later. She wasn't enough of a pal of Scarper's to keep quiet about a thing like that. Even if she didn't recognize the significance of it she would have mentioned it as something peculiar."

"I agree," Dorset said. "I just wanted support."

"And there is still one reason. There was someone else on that plane who was willing to help Scarper – for certain reasons."

"Margaret Derby Smythe? I don't know what her reasons would be. Scarper was trying to blackmail her, according to the information I have."

"I wasn't thinking of her," I said.

I went to the bedside table and riffled through the telephone book. Mrs. H.J. Smythe lived at 107 Sunnyside Place.

"How about Ann?" Dorset asked.

"What do you mean?"

"Why did you come here in such a rush to see her after things had come to a climax out at the Lakeshore? Were you afraid for her safety? Why?"

"Not particularly afraid."

"Well – did you think she was the murderer, then?"

"Sure," I said. "After all, she's a logical for Carol's murder. She killed Carol and then knocked herself out beside the corpse to throw us off the track. As for the Senator's murder, know how she did that?"

"No," Dorset grunted. Deadpan.

"She was on the plane disguised as the pilot."

"Heh," Dorset said, showing just how amused he was.

I opened the door. "Well, good-bye."

"Where are you going?"

"Looking for Ann. I'll be back."

"I won't be here."

"I won't be back here," I said, to be irritating.

He was a remarkable even-tempered old boy. "Where will you be?" he asked patiently.

"At my apartment, probably in about an hour. Will you go there and wait for me?"

"I'll go there in an hour and wait thirty minutes. Then I'll start hunting for you."

"Judging by past experience in this case, it might be a good idea," I admitted. I gave him my spare key and slouched out.

Riley climbed the tortuous Westmount hills as easily as an arrow arching away from the bow. We came to Sunnyside Place and by watching our numbers came to rest in front of what had to be No. 107.

It was another dark house.

And me without my gun. Scarper had probably thrown it in the lake.

I opened the boot of the Riley and took a half-inch ring key out of the tool kit – a slim-shanked wrench, but heavy and with a sizeable knobly end. I started up the front walk.

This was a rather modest castle – not more than forty feet across the front, about four storeys high and only deep enough for seven or eight rooms on each floor. It was red brick and light stone trim, with a front door the size of one-half the Lachine canal lift-bridge.

A light went on in the room to the right of the front door. More from surprise than anything else I dived into a shrub. I was lucky. I lost half the lobe of my left ear, but both eyes were all right. It was a prickly shrub with thorns the size of hatpins.

I said two or three responses from the black mass and came out again. It was dark enough out here so no one in a lighted room would see me. I went close to the lighted window.

There was a red-haired girl standing in the center of the room. You couldn't see any bands on her teeth, but that was because she had her mouth closed.

If she was alone, everything was all right. If she was there with someone else, I had to get her out. Anyway you looked at it, I had to go in.

I went to the front door, and it was unlocked. I went in. Ann was watching me as I came to the doorway of the lighted room. She looked a little frightened, but not very much. She noticed the wrench in my hand.

"Social call?" She asked me.

"Sure," I said. "Like you." I threw the wrench at a padded chair. It left a black slash of grease across the light upholstery where it landed.

"Aren't you through with this case yet?"

"No, aren't you?" I asked.

"I? I'm not on any case! I came here to see Margaret."

"She doesn't appear to be here. I'll take you home."

"Thank you, I'm expecting her to arrive any minute. I'll wait. If you don't mind."

I went over to a chesterfield and sat down. "I'll wait too, then. I want to see her."

"What business have you with her?"

"I have come sad news to break. Her first love is dead."

She ran her tongue nervously over her deep red lips. "You mean – Scarper. My Father."

"Sure."

"I suppose you killed him?" she asked.

"I was spared the trouble. One of his own evil companions cut him down just before he got me."

"All right," Ann said. "I'll tell her."

"She can have her letters back," I said, "if she wants to go to Scarper's house and find them."

"What do you mean?"

"You know what I mean, or you wouldn't be here."

She sat down suddenly in a large chair. "I'm here ... just to see Margaret," she almost whispered.

I pulled out the State Express, slowly extracted one from the pack, and lit up. I let her stew.

Then I said, "That story about Scarper blackmailing Margaret. I suppose she thought that was the easiest one to tell you. It explained her agitation, it would explain mysterious meetings with a man. When did you find out it was a fake?"

She shook her head miserably.

"All right, don't talk," I said. "It doesn't matter. There's still one more tangled end to be cleaned up before the final blow-off on this case. I don't need to know what you know, yet. I probably have the right to lead myself now anyway."

She stood up and came toward me. It was wonderful, the way she walked; an unlearned, unconscious grace, not like the swiveling strut of showgirls or the practiced undulation of bar girls, but more full of promise than either.

She looked down at me and said, "Margaret didn't kill anyone. You understand that, don't you? You know that?"

"You will admit, won't you, that things aren't always what they appear to you?" I asked her mildly. "People you think are sensible and normal can be ... maybe silly is the best word. Maybe almost a little bit crazy."

"Yes, I think Margaret is awfully silly," she said. "Nothing more than that."

"I hope not," I said.

"Of course not!"

"Oh, what are we talking about?" I asked wearily. "Does either of us know? I'm going. You'd better come with me."

"I'll wait for Margaret," she said definitely.

"All right."

I got up and left. I wondered if that was wise. Then I figured it was almost certain nothing would happen to her now.

Nothing would happen, because Scarper was dead.

Scene Twenty-Four

I LEFT RILEY in the big basement garage of my apartment block and went in through the fire door to the main corridor, padding across the neat grey terrazzo that the janitor swabbed every other day. I pushed the button for the self-service elevator that always worked and it came and carried me smoothly up to my floor. Then I went down another clean, smooth terrazzo corridor with washed walls of a mild, live light brown until I came to my apartment door.

I thanked God, maybe a little perfunctorily, but sincerely, that I lived in a nice place like this.

Then I thanked God again that there was something I could thank God for in this profession of mine. The detective business got me these quarters. There was nothing much else good I could say about it at the moment.

I was beat up, brassed off, tired out, hung over, and a little bit vomitous regarding life in general. I was approaching the inevitable end of a case that would leave a bad taste in my mouth for a covey of years. It might even ruin my life, what there was left to ruin.

I put the five thumbs of my left hand into a pocket and dragged out my keys and let myself in. Lights were on in my apartment, and I remembered I'd given Dorset the other key.

I went into the front room and sat down opposite him.

"Well?" he said.

"Well."

"What now?"

"We wait. She'll come here."

"How long," he asked politely, "do you think it will take?"

"Have a drink and stop worrying," I advised him.

"I don't know about you, but I'm here on business."

I gave the best imitation of a ghostly laugh I could drag up out of an empty stomach. "I'm here for pleasure, ha ha," I said, and went shambling to the kitchen. This was an evening for the big glass. I got it down again, played eenie-meenie-minie Isaac with the bottles and came to rest at the Bacardi. I fixed up six ounces of Bacardi, one whole lemon, juiced, and about half a Coke. I went back into the living room and told Dorset, "There's ginger ale, and if you want some you can get it.

He just sat.

The doorbell rang. It was bound to.

I went to let her in. She didn't look so hot.

She had been crying and worrying about things in general, and her face had the general appearance of a ploughed field crows had been walking around in. A pity, because it was a lovely face.

I ushered her in, and at the door of the living room she stopped short. She had suddenly seen the bulgy, rumpled figure of the Dorset sprawled on my chartreuse chesterfield. And that was something she hadn't expected.

Dorset got slowly to his big feet. The old Indian-chaser look was in his eyes. He wasn't going to waste time with preliminaries. The overburdened, cautious, sagging, old frame straightened up into a semblance of the old disciplined days when he wore the proudest uniform on earth.

"Miss Malone," I said, "I believe you know Inspector Dorset."

This was his moment.

"Good evening—" he paused "Miss Scarper."

This was his moment, he thought. I felt pretty sorry for him.

"Won't you sit down," he told Maida. I guided her to one of the overstuffed chartreuse chairs.

Dorset picked up one of the straight side chairs from beside the wall and came and sat directly in front of Maida. I stood beside her.

"Why did you come here, Miss Scarper?"

"I ... I ..." she tried, but couldn't bring anything else out. She watched him with her deep, green-blue eyes full of deadly fright.

Dorset leaned toward her. He looked at her steadily, but this was no grilling, no psychological third degree. He spoke quietly and rather slowly.

"I have a long story to tell you," he said. "I want you to listen very patiently and carefully, if you will. Then I want you to tell me just what you think of it."

I went over to the mantel and found my six-ounce Bacardi. It still had about four ounces left. I brought it back and moistened my throat a few times.

Dorset said, "On Flight 93, out of LaGuardia last Monday night, a man was killed. A very important man. At first it wasn't even certain that his death was not accidental, because there was no obvious weapon carried by any of those on the plane. But a careful postmortem examination of the wound suggested what might have caused it. And we found that one of the detachable chair arms in the plane cabin showed the expected traces. Senator Kelloway had been struck with the end of that arm."

Maida was staring, mesmerized, into his eyes.

"It was an ingenious and brutal murder. It was done by an opportunist, on the spur of the moment, because circumstances were perfect – the trip rough, the passengers all sick, the plane dark. But, as I pointed out to Teed once before, that didn't mean it was an unpremeditated murder. No, the Senator was not a man one would murder without deep and long-standing cause. Only the method of the murder was unpremeditated. A deep hatred of him, or a compelling emotion connected with someone he also was connected with, lay behind the murder.

"That meant we had to look into the lives of everyone who had traveled on the plane that night, to unearth the cause of Kelloway's killing. I will tell you what we found. First of all, we were able to eliminate five people completely. Carles Garnett, the press agency editor; Aime LaRouche, the salesman; Florence Milsky, the Bronx office girl; the co-pilot and the pilot. As far as we were able to discover – and we combed exceedingly fine – they had no connection with Senator Kelloway nor with anyone who knew him."

Dorset paused. Without taking his eyes off Maida he drew a scuffed, dull-bowled old pipe from his pocket. He sucked it experimentally, and it gurgled. Absently, so immersed in his story that he forgot where he was, he shook it out. The dark drops of tarry tobacco juice glistened on the pile of the green rug.

"We were left with seven people to investigate more fully. Mr. Teed and Mr. Willcot we dropped almost immediately. Each of them had, in a sense, an unemotional connection with Kelloway; a business connection that they could terminate when they wished, that did not call for the radical measure of murder.

"Now we had five. The five were Isaac Scarper and four people linked in various ways to him. Horatio White, whom he had used. Lorette Toledo, apparently a casual acquaintance. Mrs. Smythe, a woman who once had loved him. And yourself – his daughter."

Dorset paused to see how he was getting along. He was producing no particular reaction. She was sitting there staring at him, frightened but waiting. Just waiting. Dorset sighed and dropped his eyes to his shoes. "I think I'd like that drink now, Mr. Teed," he said mildly. I went to the kitchen and poured him three ounces of Berry's Best, with water, and brought it back. He had waited.

"You can guess the first one we eliminated," Dorset went on. "We wrote off Scarper himself. He had about the poorest opportunity of anyone on the plane, considering that he was sitting with someone and was quite far away from the Senator. We crossed Lorette Toledo off the list because she was not intimately enough concerned with either Scarper or the Senator to commit murder. And we crossed off the colored minister, Horatio White, because of his distance from the Senator, because he was so sick, and because of his general character. Later, the manner of Horatio's own death confirmed our judgment there."

He sipped slowly at his drink, studying Maida. I wondered what he thought he could do by this recital.

"You will ask: why did we suspect these people, merely because they were associated with Scarper? The reason grew from our knowledge of why Kelloway made his trip to New York. He had gone to get evidence against Scarper, whom he hated. And he had found enough to ruin Scarper. Then perhaps, since no one directly tied to the Senator was a good suspect, the Senator was killed to protect Scarper. Killed by someone under Scarper's control – like Horatio White – or by someone who loved him and wanted desperately to keep him from harm.

"Who loved him? Margaret Smythe? She had loved him once, but now he was taking advantage of that to blackmail her. She hated him. And you, Maida Malone, what about you?"

He paused once more, but getting no response went immediately on. "Your mother uses her maiden name, which she gave to you also. That is because her husband, your father, deserted you both and left you to struggle alone. But is it not true that despite herself she still loves that man? Is it not true she taught you he was weak rather than wicked? Did she not tell you over and over that your father was a great man, a man you could be proud of, who left her through her fault more than his? Did you not meet and become friends with this man, your father? And is it not true that he is – Isaac Scarper?"

Maida wept in a wrenching burst of sobbing that shook her out of her glazed stare, her frozen half-hypnotized stillness. She collapsed across the arm of the chair, racked with the sobs.

Dorset watched. Then he got up from his chair, still looking at her. He shrugged wearily. For the first time he raised the drink to his lips. He drank thirstily. He fumbled in his pocked and brought out a big wooden kitchen match and tried to light his pipe. At last it caught and he puffed it easily. He had slumped again and the tension and stiffness were all gone out of him.

He thought it was through.

I tended Maida first. I made another trip to the kitchen for the usual purpose. I pulled out the Hennessey and filled a shot glass. I came back and forced her face gently up from the shelter of her arms. Her hands clung tightly to her eyes and her face was drawn down long, and flushed, and shaking. She hid it as best she could. I fed her the brandy, carefully. She fought it, but it flowed between her lips and she gagged and swallowed and then became quiet.

She sat upright in the chair again, one hand to her forehead, hiding the deep intense mystery of her eyes. I thought about the calm depths of those eyes, the soft sweetness of her rippling brogue, the warmth of her body against mine. I took my drink and drained it.

I had a terribly unpleasant thing to do, and I had to do it and get it over.

"Dorset!"

My voice was sharp, and he turned to me with a puzzled scowl. Maida let her hand fall and watched me.

"You can't get a confessions out of anyone when you start with the wrong information. I know you want to break this case. I know and you know that you could only convict Maida on her own admission of guilt, because there's no conclusive evidence. But she'll never admit the wrong story."

Dorset went to the chesterfield and sat down. Now it was his turn to listen and wait.

"Isaac Scarper and Maida's mother never met," I said. "As a matter of fact, Maida never saw Scarper before that night on the plane. In other words, he wasn't her father, at all. I was wrong when I first thought Kelloway was Ann Wedgewood's father. This time, you were wrong."

I'd moistened my throat enough to be able to use a cigarette. I got one going. "I talked to Miss Malone – Senior – a little while ago. She told me her former husband was dead. Her former lover, she meant – she kept the name Malone for a good reason. It was still legally hers, even after Maida was born.

"And that night on the plane, something a little amazing happened. Maida's a nurse. She's seen death until it means almost nothing. But she wept for Kelloway."

I puffed hard and threw the butt viciously at the fireplace. "She wept for her father."

It was time to turn to Maida. My eyes fastened on hers. "You weren't like Ann, a girl who knew no father. Your mother had told you about Kelloway. Then, the first time you saw him, he died before your eyes."

I was shouting at her now. "And you wept. From pity?

Or for what you had done? Here was the man who'd deserted your mother, refused to give her his name, left her to make her own way with a babe. Made your childhood a succession of shabby rooms in cheap houses on slum streets. Were you swept away by your hatred and rage at him when you first saw him there? Did you pick up that weapon in the dimness and strike a blow for all those years, all that had happened to your mother and you? Did you kill him?"

She screamed.

Her tension had been mounting, her eyes widening until the whites showed above the iris, her hands clawing at nothing, her mouth drawing open in a gargoyle grimace. Then the scream.

It left her limp, her head bowed, arms akimbo.

"You can go," I said.

Her head rose slowly and she looked at me. She didn't understand.

"Go, leave," I said. "The Inspector isn't armed. He won't stop you. My revolver's sitting on a hook in the hall closet. No one will stop you. Go home. Think over what you have to do now."

She got up like someone in a dream and wandered away from us. Dorset edged to the brink of his seat, a look of utter amazement on his face. He knew something was up. He didn't know what.

She opened a door. It wasn't the front door of the apartment. It was the hall closet door.

When she came back the gun was pointed directly at my chest. It wavered for a minute to Dorset, and then came back to me.

"I must make you believe," she whispered. "I must make you believe me, or I shall have to kill you. Kill you both."

One hand went to her head and brushed the long, shining black hair back from her eyes. "A nightmare," she said softly. "Like a nightmare, all of it, since that night on the plane. You see, Scarper thought this too. He thought I had killed the old Senator. He came to me the very next day – early, before I had seen anyone else. He said he knew I had killed. He said I must kill once more, kill for him, or he would give me away. So hard and so vainly I protested. He told me to go to Carol Kelloway and murder her. Then, he said, I would be safe."

"But ... ?" I prompted.

"I kept denying. He told me that the Senator was my father, and that I had killed my father, and that now I must do away with Carol or I would never escape. I don't know what more he said. I remember nothing but that I cried and wept and at last he went away."

"Why the umbrella?" I asked.

"I was so afraid you would think the same thing. The thing you do think now. And after Carol was killed I was horrified beyond reason. I was foolish to come and lie to you but I did not dare do anything other."

"I don't believe you," I said harshly. "Go ahead. Shoot me. Make it three."

At last there was something plain to see in her eyes that had been so obscure. There was fear. She stared at me and then her eyes dropped to the revolver in her hand. She watched it, fascinated, as it dropped from her limp fingers to the floor. Then she sank in a little heap beside it, completely unconscious.

Dorset's clenched jaw relaxed and his pipe fell to the rug and bounced twice in little erratic curves. The breath he had been holding for three or four minutes burst out and nearly blew a copy of *Fortune* off the coffee table.

I picked up the gun and tossed it to him. "It's all right,"

I said. "The shells for it are in the second drawer to the left of the record player."

Dorset descended to slang. "Now you tell me!" he wheezed.

I picked up Maida and took her into my bedroom. I opened the window wide and laid her on my bed. Then I returned to Dorset.

"Brutal, but effective," I said. "God, I hated to do that. But I doubt if you would have ever fully believed if it had been done any simpler way."

"Believed what?"

"That she didn't do any murder."

"Now, don't tell me –"

"She was telling the truth," I snorted at him. "Do you think she wouldn't have pulled the trigger otherwise? The murders we have now were done by a maniac. A maniac wouldn't stop at two more."

"Then who—?"

"You suspected her because of her umbrella story, didn't you? And you built up an elaborate guess about Scarper being her father, to explain the whole thing. You hoped she'd break down and confess. But she didn't, because it wasn't the right explanation. There are too many explanations, plausible or possible, to this. Mine wasn't the right one either, of course. But I had to prove that. To myself, probably, as much as to you – because it could have happened my way."

"How *did* it happen?"

"You were right almost down to the last step. You eliminated all of them but two. But then you picked wrong."

"Margaret Smythe?"

"Sure."

"Good God, no! Why?"

"Who knows how a crazy woman's brain works? I guessed it the way you did, just by elimination. But I eliminated Maida."

"How?"

"I guess ... just because I knew her better than you did."

"And then?"

"Things kept fitting in. Finally I located Ann tonight and found that she was worried about Margaret. She had found out her mother still loved Scarper. I almost made her admit it."

"It was the chair arm from Margaret's seat that did the murder," Dorset admitted. "I couldn't believe she had done it. I thought she had removed it to sleep, and Maida had picked it up and used it."

"Margaret was just ahead of Kelloway in the plane, and across the aisle. She didn't even have to leave her seat to do it. Ridiculously simple and quick."

"But ... Carol. With her head nearly severed. And if Margaret did that, she stunned Ann as well."

"Anyone else would probably have killed Ann. Margaret just put her out long enough to get away."

"But ... I was as hideous a killing as I've seen."

"Sure. Scarper was a hideous little creature. After what Maida said, you can hardly doubt that he made Margaret do it. Probably he even suggested the method. She was enough in love with him to kill Kelloway, just to protect him. I wonder what she thought when he asked her to kill Carol? But I doubt if she was thinking at all."

"Her story was that Scarper was blackmailing her to get control of her husband's share of the titanium interests."

"That was her story. She went to New York to meet him to arrange a way she could get the interests for him.

There was no blackmail, unless it was when he accused her of the first murder and forced her into the second."

"But why did she tell that blackmail story? Why tell it to Ann?"

"To explain a sudden trip to New York, meetings with an unknown man. To explain her nervousness and tension that came from a reunion with the man she still loved."

Dorset shook his head, still only half believing. "Now what?" he asked finally.

"Wait a little longer. I wasn't really expecting Maida at all. I was expecting someone else."

I walked out and took the latch off the apartment door. I went into the kitchen and poured the rest of the Bacardi bottle into my glass. I didn't check on how much it was. I didn't care. There were still bad things to come.

I came back to the living room and stood before the fireplace waiting.

The apartment door burst open and Ann ran into the room. Her fire-red hair was disheveled as though she had fought her way through thick underbrush. Her dress was torn where it had caught against some projection.

She ran into my arms. I didn't even have time to put the drink down. It splintered on the hearth.

She held me tightly. She was sobbing. The words tumbled out. "I waited ... waited for her so long, but she didn't come. Then I went upstairs in the dark. I put her light on, Russ. She was there, on her bed. I don't know what it was she'd taken. She must have been lying there, dead, when we both came into the house."

I pressed her head against my shoulder and soothed her. I scowled at Dorset and he got up slowly and silently and went away.

Her sobs were strong and deep. They would help her. But it would be a long time before all this left her, a long time before she could forget. After this night she would not want to see me again, or see Montreal, until much time had passed.

It would be a long time, but I wanted to wait.

THE END